DOWN RIVER

BOOKS FOR BOYS

by Richard Church

DOWN RIVER
FIVE BOYS IN A CAVE

RICHARD CHURCH

DOWN RIVER

THE JOHN DAY COMPANY NEW YORK

CONTENTS

DOWN RIVER

I.

AN INVITATION

Jᴏʜɴ Wᴀʟᴛᴇʀs had a letter from his doctor uncle George during the Christmas holidays.

You will remember [it said] that when you explored those caves by the bend of the river during the summer vacation last year, you found a human skull? I followed your route a week or two later, thanks to the map which you made and left with me, and I took the skull to the County Museum. I heard no more until last week. An expert from London has been down to examine it, and the verdict is that the skull is definitely Roman, from about the fourth century A.D., when Rome ruled Britain.

How it got there nobody can guess. The Romans had garrisons all along the western borders of the area they controlled, but no settling was done so far into the Celtic retreats beyond, for isolated Roman villas and farms would not have been safe. This fellow might have been exploring, as you and your friends were; or he might have been fugitive, after committing a crime, and so cut off from his fellows. Whatever the cause, there he ended his days. I've had no time to explore further. There may be other relics. Why don't you come next summer and have a look around? Your aunt seconds this motion. I believe she's got a soft spot for you.

By the way, things have gone from bad to worse next door, and the Reynolds family has broken up. Your friend George took a hard knock over this and Aunt Mary has offered to adopt him so that he can continue at school, where he's been doing fairly well. He needs a bit of feeding up, too. I don't think his mother (now departed) was keen on cooking. At any rate, he's bringing his clothes and things in to us this week, and henceforth will be a member of the family, making three in all. I've got no objection. I took to him that night you brought him to supper last year. Think about my suggestion, while Aunt Mary writes to your people. Is your brother too young to come too?

John Walters knew that his uncle was a busy doctor, with no time for writing long letters. This occasion must therefore be a special one. Six months ahead was a long time to span. But the thought of searching those caves again made John so excited that his spectacles steamed up, and he had to take them off and wipe them before he could continue reading his uncle's letter.

At first he was against taking his brother Andrew, two years his junior and rather a ruffian. John was beginning to take archeology seriously, and his active mind immediately began to make plans for a really scientific attack on the caves. Andrew would be a hindrance to any methodical work. Also the members of the Tomahawk Gang might object.

John decided to say nothing to Andrew until he had thought things out more clearly. It might be a good idea to seek his parents' views on the suggestion from Uncle George.

But events moved faster than John's thoughts. He heard a scuffle down the stairs, and a moment later the dining-room door was burst open, almost ruining the lock, to admit a shock-headed boy in a torn dressing gown—Andrew!

He was wild with excitement, and John saw the flushed cheeks, the eyes flashing, the lips contorted by a crowd of words all trying to tumble out together.

"It's by the sea!" he spluttered at last. "And I'm coming too! I'm going surf riding, like the South Sea Islanders!"

After that, John had to give in. It would have been cruelty to animals to dampen such enthusiasm. He knew, too, that Andrew had been lonely last year, staying with grandparents who were very strict, with no other children in the house, and the house in a sleepy old suburb of London. Andrew's excitement made John feel ashamed of his dog-in-the-manger mood. With a sigh, he submitted to the responsibility of taking Andrew next summer.

"You'll need a haircut," he said, forgetting that the holiday was six months ahead. And you'll have to lend a hand, for there'll be some work to do."

Andrew crowed with delight. "Lend a hand! Lend a hand!" he echoed, putting a tune to the words and jigging up and down, "Lend a foot! Lend a leg, lend a—" But John had to slap him down before he broke something on the breakfast table.

At that point, their mother appeared and the conversation took a calmer turn. It also clinched the proposal for Andrew to go with John to Uncle George's in the summer.

2.

SIX MONTHS LATER

By the time the summer holidays loomed
slowly ahead the brothers were almost ill with excitement. Andrew had changed since Christmas. His head
was too big for his body, and no matter how often he
was sent to the barber his hair remained tousled, standing up like a busby. And as it was dark, and his quick-
darting eyes were black, the boys at school nicknamed
him Tadpole. The name stuck, and was used also at
home—except by his mother, who thought it undigni-
fied, and a reflection upon her.

So it was John Walters, the Tadpole in his tow, who
was seen off at Paddington Station one hot morning at
the end of July. Both parents came to the ceremony, for
they too were going for a holiday, an automobile tour
in the Scottish Highlands. Father was therefore in a
lively mood, and John, looking at him as he stood on
the platform by the door of the railway car, saw in this
usually severe personage a sudden likeness to Uncle

George, that paragon of grownups, the doctor and ex-mountaineer.

"Take care of *that* object!" said Father to John, pointing his chin at the Tadpole, a smile on his face, but a gleam of seriousness in his eyes. "See that he washes from time to time."

The Tadpole scowled. He had lately begun to suspect that Father spent too much time pulling his leg. That left him stranded, with only his mother to turn to; and she was inclined to fuss over his health. She was doing it now. "Don't let him catch cold bathing, John," she whispered, but not quietly enough to prevent Andrew from hearing.

He snorted and slapped his brother's knee with the window strap, as though to warn him off.

Then the whistle sounded, and the parents began to shrink to pygmy size as the train slid out of the great dome and the platforms narrowed, joined, disappeared. The boys, leaning out of the window, saw a speck of white—Mother's handkerchief. Then it was lost in the smoke.

Nothing much happened; but there was more than enough to look at, as on all train journeys. Soon after they had passed Reading, a man in the opposite corner, who had been dozing after reading a racing paper, looked across and offered John a cigarette.

"What! You don't smoke?" he jeered. "You're not

half a man! Mind if I do?" But he was already puffing away, though the boys' mother had insisted on putting them in a non-smoking compartment.

John glanced at the label on the window, the man saw this glance and grinned again, showing a gold tooth. He flicked his fingers, and a ring, with a bright stone in it, flashed.

"Going to the races?" he said.

John decided not to reply. He didn't like the look of this character. It wasn't the fact that he ignored the convenience of other passengers, or that the gold tooth and the gaudy ring repelled the boy. It was the glassy fishy eyes that aroused suspicion.

At that moment the ticket inspector looked in from the corridor, guiding an old lady who had been smoked out of an adjoining compartment. He saw the racy gentleman, summed him up, and suggested that he should change seats with the passenger who had just left a smoking compartment. With an ill grace, and some muttering, the man got up and disappeared.

"Some people—!" said the inspector, while he clipped the tickets. He nodded in disgust, saying, as he slid the door along, "Anybody meeting you young gentlemen?"

John knew the ropes, however, having done the journey alone a year ago, when he was only thirteen. And he had a good memory, being a methodical chap. So all went well, including two offerings of chocolate from the old lady, who chatted to them sensibly all the way to Bath, where they were met by Aunt Mary in her small runabout station wagon, a new feature with which the Tadpole fell so violently in love that he hardly bothered to greet his aunt. So she left him to it, for the time being, and gave her attention to John.

As they made northward, to the hills and the coast, she inquired about the family and events of the past year.

"Much has been happening since you were with us, John. Uncle told you in his letter about that skull you found. Somebody has written a paper about it, a specialist from London. He didn't mention how it came to light, so I pointed this out, and he added that it was found by some schoolboys. I said that all boys are schoolboys, and that if it had been unearthed by a party of Members of Parliament would he have said that it was 'found by some politicians'? In the end he gave your names, all five of you."

Here the Tadpole interrupted to ask how many miles an hour the station wagon could do in top gear. After he had been satisfied, Aunt Mary resumed.

"Uncle George seemed not to approve, but I said fair's fair. The boys' good job of work, and the fact that they did not disturb the site, ought to be acknowledged."

Then she added, after pausing to negotiate a turning

16

off the hill where a tradesman's van was standing and blocking the clear view, "By the way, whose idea was it that you should leave the skull untouched, just as you found it? A sensible idea; very scientific."

John didn't like to tell, for he thought he might be showing off. Besides, after the lapse of nearly a year, he was not quite sure of the details. But he was practically certain that it was he who had insisted on not touching the skull, though one of the Tomahawk Gang, that little chap whom they had called Lightning because he was so impulsive, had wanted to bring the find out of the cave.

As they approached the thirty-mile speed limit on the outskirts of the town by the Severn estuary, where Uncle George practiced, they were nearly involved in an accident. Aunt Mary had made her signal before pulling out to pass a slow-moving eight-wheeler. She had almost reached it when there was a loud hoot from a car behind. Startled, she pulled in again behind the heavy truck. Instantly the following car swung around her, over the white line, and dashed on. There was a shrieking of brakes and tires from a smart black sedan coming toward this dangerous little group, followed by a scraping—a mere touch, but enough to frighten everybody. The new car pulled up, and the offending overtaker did the same. John saw that it was an old sports car, large and dilapidated. Sitting in the back, behind two other men, was the man with the flashy ring and the fishy eye. He was looking out over the back of the open car, grinning. There was no mistaking that cocky grin, with the snarl behind it.

John had no time to look again, for after a burst of laughter the three men drove on, the old sports car trembling, its loose fender flapping, the exhaust roaring through a broken pipe.

The eight-wheeler had pulled up, its driver having seen the incident reflected in his driving mirror. Mrs. Walters stopped behind him, and both got out to go over to the new black sedan, which had a red number plate slung over the permanent one. The indignant driver, hot in the face, got out to inspect the damage. A long smearing scratch, an inch or two wide, ran down the front and rear door panels. Fortunately the body work was not dented.

"I was doing under thirty, driving this new car to a customer. I'll ask you to vouch for what happened, if you'll be kind enough. Us chaps usually get the blame."

"Sure enough, chum," said the truck driver, offering him a cigarette. "I saw it coming. You recognize these flash boys a mile away. I'll bet that old boy is a public danger anyway. I had a good view of his number, though. It's ZX8080—easy to see, easy to remember. I'll report it, first speed cop I see. You do the same."

"And I don't need to ask for your address, ma'am,"

said the ill-used mechanic, "I'm on the doctor's panel." Reassured by this certainty of evidence in his favor, he exchanged notes with the truck driver, a long-distance man, got into the disfigured sedan, and turned to follow the others back into the town and his garage.

"I expected those toughs to try to put the blame on me," said Aunt Mary, after she had got clear of the truck. "They look that sort."

John then told her about the man in the train.

"Yes, that's the kind of character," she said. "A menace to society. Nobody's safe from them. But it doesn't do to dwell on other people's faults too much, eh John?"

They drove through the town to the northern end, where the coast curved in to the small mouth of the little river that flowed into the great estuary, making a peninsula under the shelter of the rocky hills along the farther bank, to the northeast. The doctor's house stood in the residential area halfway up that peninsula, the garden running down to the river, which flowed behind the narrow copse backing the lawn and vegetable garden, and extended through the fence to hide the next-door garden from the stream.

"Uncle told you about George Reynolds?" asked Aunt Mary, as they turned into the short drive. "He's one of us now, John, after a lot of unhappiness. He's taking up drawing and painting in a big way, and we intend to send him to the Art School when he's finished at the

Grammar. You'll be surprised when you see what he's been doing."

"No, I shan't," said John, opening the car door for his aunt. "I haven't forgotten our adventure last year, and how he showed up then. It'll be good to see him again."

He didn't want to ask about the trouble to which his uncle and aunt had referred. Instead, he looked at the house, and from the house to his aunt, who had taken Andrew by the hand, thinking perhaps that he might be feeling shy, or lost, or tired after the long journey by train and car. But Andrew still could not take his attention from the new station wagon, and he wanted to linger near it. He showed no desire to go indoors, or even to glance at the outside of the house which he was visiting for the first time.

Aunt Mary was amused and waited patiently, smiling down at him. Then she observed that John was studying her through his spectacles.

"What are you so solemn about?" she said, a hand on his shoulder.

"I was thinking, Aunt Mary. You look years younger than you did last summer."

Then he turned to the house, and added, "Everything is smaller than I remembered it. Whatever has happened?"

"You're growing and catching up on the rest of the

20

world. You always were an old-fashioned party, John. It must be those gold-rimmed spectacles!"

She was laughing at him. But he didn't mind. Aunt Mary was that kind of person; something impersonal about her, like warm summer weather.

At that moment, a very thin, lanky figure came from the back of the house, around by the rose garden, carrying an easel, paint box, and a folding stool. Seeing John, he hesitated, stood still, almost turned back.

"George!" cried Aunt Mary. He could not retreat. John saw him afresh, a different boy, but the same. He recalled the absurd figure in the over-large mackintosh, distorted by hidden coils of rope ladder and other gear, with whom he had set out on that morning in September nearly a year ago. Here was the same George Reynolds, still littered with things to carry: and likely to be.

It was odd that this apparition should be the only thing to lure Andrew away from the new car. The small boy turned at once, his dark eyes interested, and he approached Reynolds as though stalking big game, fascinated.

"This is John's brother," said Aunt Mary. And as she spoke, both John and Reynolds realized that they had not said a word to greet each other. In a way, they had to start afresh. Or did it mean that they were carrying on where they had left off last year?

3.

THE TOMAHAWK CLUB
REVIVES

U<small>NCLE</small> G<small>EORGE</small> was out, doing his turn at "surgery hour" in the clinic downtown. Aunt Mary, leaving the car for the doctor to put it away—and also for Andrew to work off his infatuation by sitting in it, alone, entranced—went to the kitchen to prepare the evening meal, her daily help having gone home long since.

John and George were thus left together. They were both uncomfortable. What had happened next door, in the Reynolds home, lay between them, and neither of the boys knew how to climb that barrier.

"Let's go to my room," said George, after some uncertain lingering in the hall and dining room. "Then we'll come back and lend Aunt Mary a hand."

John followed him up the stairs, still uncertain what line to take. George was definitely not a fellow one could be sorry for. He looked lonely, and there was something about him, as though he had been hungry for a very long time. But John found himself respecting that appearance, not pitying it.

"Want some help with those things?" he asked.

"No, you've got your bags to carry. Isn't that enough?"

George looked over his shoulder as he replied, and though the staircase was dimly lit John could see a challenge in George's eye. He decided to say nothing about the troubles. After all, they weren't anything he could mend.

John dumped his bags in the room he had occupied last year. He would now share it with Andrew, as he realized when he saw the camp bed against the farther wall. He heard George dropping things in the former guest room next door. Both rooms overlooked the garden and the copse, beyond which flowed the river.

Still Andrew had not come up, so John rejoined Reynolds, who was busy stowing his painting gear in a cupboard. He did not look around, and John was able to notice certain alterations in the room. It had been redecorated, and it now boasted a writing desk with drawers, and a bookcase with two of the four shelves still empty.

John walked over to the window. "It's the same view as from your place," he said.

"My place?" repeated George, as though he didn't understand. Then, reluctantly, he added, "Oh! Oh, yes.

The same view." He frowned as he spoke, and again John felt uncomfortable. He was miserable too. This was going to be grim, and no sort of holiday!

Suddenly George smiled, and joined John at the window. "Let's face it!" he said. "Things aren't the same as last year. They couldn't be worse than they were then. I don't want my family discussed, that's all. If we get the Club together, I don't want any remarks."

"You mean from Alan Hobbs, I suppose?" said John quietly. He had cheered up. It was good to get this trouble out of the way right at the beginning. "Nobody else is likely to say anything, surely?"

"I suppose not," said George, doubtfully. "Maybe I'm still a bit sore. You know—you know—" His voice broke, and John stared hard through the window, afraid to look at the struggle going on inside that thin, lanky figure and behind that rather grim face. But instantly George regained command of himself. "You see," he went on, "Aunt and Uncle have done this for me." He looked around the comfortable room—*his* room. "And all the rest of it. They've tried to put things right. That's what I'm trying to say, John."

"Shut up," said John. "D'you think I don't know? Let's get on with things. I'm sorry my young brother has had to tag along. He's a bit young, and very wild, but we'll have to bring him into the Club."

"Well, there's one vacancy," said George.

24

"What d'you mean?"

"Alan Hobbs!"

They looked at each other, and knew that the barrier was down.

"Yes," said George. "He went off to boarding school last autumn term after the summer holidays. He'd forgotten us all when he came home for Christmas."

"Perhaps things rankled," said John.

"He hadn't anything to be proud of after that showdown in the caves."

"Maybe," said George, brooding. "And what's more, his old man seems to be more prosperous than ever. They've bought the house next door, and—"

"What, *your* house?"

"Well, it wasn't ours any longer. When the break-up came, everything was sold. Old Hobbs bought it later, and has been doing it up inside and out. He's even rebuilt the old boathouse where we first planned the expedition into the caves. And he's got a motor speedboat in it now."

"And what about Alan?"

"What d'you expect? When I told him you were coming down, and that we intended to call the Tomahawk Club together again, for further exploration where we found the skull, he looked very funny, and said, 'Where *I* found the skull, you mean!' So I reminded him that it was you who spotted it."

"What did he say to that?"

"He asked what proof we'd got!"

John whistled, and the two faithful members of the Club looked at each other in silence for a moment, while this ugly bit of news sank in. George continued, tapping the window ledge thoughtfully with a pencil.

"I left him that one, and asked about calling the Club together. 'I don't know,' said Hobbs, 'I'll have to think about it. You make these claims. It seems to me there's a lack of loyalty in that little gang. I may have to reconstitute the Club, or make other arrangements.' Yes, that's how it stands, John. He knows how to put us in the wrong. It takes my breath away; at least, when it comes to talking!"

They stared gloomily and angrily at each other.

"What's he mean by that? Making other arrangements, didn't you say?"

"Yes, I wonder too. It sounds like a threat."

"Well," said John, more cheerfully, "we had a sample of his threats last year, in the caves, didn't we? And what came of that?"

George grinned. They both recalled the picture of Alan Hobbs on his knees, crying and refusing to go home after the loss of the big electric lamp which he had borrowed without permission from his father.

Further discussion was interrupted by Aunt Mary,

who knocked at the open door, and asked if she could come in.

George turned eagerly and stepped forward to greet her. She appeared, with young Andrew entangled in her skirt, pressing backward because he was bewildered or shy. Even so, he gave the impression that this would quickly wear off.

"D'you like George's room?" Aunt Mary asked John. He did not reply, but they looked at each other swiftly, happily, knowing what it all meant.

Andrew now began to ask questions. He poked about, examining George's possessions, inquiring how *this* worked, what *that* was for, why George carried a short stick with a wash-leather knob when he went painting. The two older boys had the impression that his large head with its busby of hair would surely get stuck in something. George answered the quick-fire questions patiently, studying the small boy from time to time with an indulgent humor.

"Tadpole, be seen and not heard!" whispered John several times during the early evening; but the urchin commanded most of the attention and conversation until Uncle George appeared, just as Aunt Mary was dishing up the dinner at seven o'clock.

Uncle George was a larger edition of the boys' father, and he looked much sterner. This silenced Andrew, but only for a short time. He soon discovered that Uncle George's severity was merely skin deep. By the time dinner was over he had charmed the doctor into submission, making him yet another answerer of questions and explainer of the myriad problems that filled Andrew's day between waking and sleeping. John, who shared a room with him, had frequently to deal with problems put to him in the small hours of the night, should both boys chance to waken.

John meanwhile was quick to notice how happily George Reynolds fitted into the household. He was still a quiet, retiring soul, but John saw that behind this native habit, the tall, gloomy-looking youth was happy enough. His very slowness proclaimed it, as though he wanted to arrest every moment of his new life in the Walters home, and taste it to the full, and to make sure that such security could be true.

Next morning, at breakfast, John inquired about something which had been puzzling him since he learned of the loss of the boathouse belonging to Reynolds' old home.

"I've seen to that," said George. "We are to meet at the Rock, at ten o'clock."

"You mean you've remembered that?" John said. "Why, it's the spot where the whole thing began. I was lying there watching a flight of rooks go over, and—"

28

"I know. But we've no time now for the whole history. It's already half past nine, so we'd better get ready. We'll need the map which you drew last year for Uncle George; and a notebook to record our plans. I've told Soames, and Meaty Sanders. They're game for anything. By the way, Lightning Soames isn't much different, though his eldest sister has got married; which leaves him with only about half a dozen elder sisters to fuss over him. He's still no bigger than your young brother, I should say. He's pretty smart, you know: older, and more sensible than he looks."

"Is it all right to bring Andrew?" asked John. He half expected George to turn down the suggestion, though nothing had been said the night before when the conduct of Alan Hobbs had been discussed.

"Why not?" said George, in surprise. John could not reply, because he was wondering whether he was pleased or not. Young brothers can be embarrassing in the company of one's equals. On the other hand, the Tadpole would be mighty lonely if left out of the Club's adventures. Like young Soames, he was a plucky little devil.

It was a somewhat subdued Andrew, however, who set out with the older couple, for John had given him a few heavy instructions to act as a curb on his excessive curiosity and daredevil lack of reverence for his seniors

—excluding, perhaps, Father, who was a Law unto Himself, and certainly rather formidable, though he looked quiet enough.

The sun was already fierce. Flies buzzed among the bracken, which stood at least a foot higher than it had been last year when John first waded through it from the road gate to the Rock, some hundred yards over the common. George led the way, turning to left, and later to right, thus to avoid making a path straight from the gate to the Rock, which would have been conspicuous from the road.

The Tadpole looked even smaller, overshadowed by the six-foot bracken. John watched him trudging on behind George, and he felt suddenly glad that the imp had not been left out of the things to come. Wondering what they were likely to be, John realized that he was almost sick with anticipation. The scene inside the caves was still clear in his memory: the narrow entrance, the curving ledge with the dangerous bit of screen; the great dome with the stalactite hanging like a chandelier; the fissure in the wall, leading to the pothole down which he and Lightning Soames had been lowered on the rope; the underground river, and the two siphons, the first of which the Club had broken through; and then the finding of the skull, at the very last moment when the explorers were about to leave the caverns by the newly found tunnel, after Alan Hobbs had funked the dive through the second siphon out to daylight.

The three boys had no sooner reached the rock, and clambered up to its flat top, than they heard a shout from the road. It was the deep voice of a man; but it came from a familiar figure, the huge bulk of "Meaty" Sanders. They saw him stoop inside the gate, and a moment later he straightened up again, with "Lightning" Soames as a flying angel on his back. The head and shoulders of this complex animal thus emerged above the top of the bracken, and two arms continued to gesticulate in excited semaphore during the passage from the gate to the rock.

Meaty deposited his burden beside the other boys, and stared up at them, puffing, while a smile like that of the rising sun shone from his sweaty face.

"Hallo!" he said, as though he had last seen John Walters an hour or two ago, instead of a year.

In an instant, Andrew transferred his allegiance from Reynolds to this mountain of good-humored flesh, bone and muscle.

"Hallo!" he chirruped in reply. "What's that you've got there?"

Meaty raised his arm, as though he had forgotten the heavy trenching tool.

"Oh, that's because I've grown since last year. I remember how I had to undress to squeeze through that tunnel at the opening. What chance do I stand now?"

His huge body shook with laughter, and everyone else laughed too, except Andrew, who was lost in one of his acts of silent worship, staring at the mighty limbs of Meaty Sanders, as he had stared at the new car the day before.

"Come along," said Meaty, reaching up and hoisting Andrew on to his shoulders. "It'll take a bit of time to widen that tunnel."

Lightning snatched the trenching tool, and led the way, threshing at the bracken to clear a path.

"Are you John's brother?" grunted Meaty, looking up at the urchin. "You don't wear glasses, then?"

"No, I'm a Red Indian. I can see in the dark. I'm a dead shot, too!"

"I'll chuck you into the bracken if you brag like that!"

This was said with such indulgent kindness that Andrew was about to stretch his imagination still further when the party reached the mountain ash tree at the hidden entrance to the cave, and the small boy was swung down to the ground and his natural height.

From this position he was able to examine Lightning Soames, and to see a person hardly bigger than himself. Oddly enough, he found this discouraging, and he contemplated the rival with shyness and suspicion. Lightning's quick wits and movements increased Andrew's cautious approach. There would have to be a show-down between them, thought John, who did not fail to notice the somewhat hostile side glances between the two smaller boys. He knew, too, that Andrew was in for trouble if he pitted himself against the superior years and cunning of Lightning Soames. But that would be a good lesson, John decided, for a cheeky young brother.

"Here goes!" cried Meaty, stripping off his coat and shirt, and taking the trenching tool from Lightning. "I'll go in first and clear that narrow passage. Look after that!" he added, dropping a haversack on top of his dis-carded garments. "It's got the grub."

He parted the undergrowth, and dived into the hole near the roots of the mountain ash tree. The other boys heard him struggling and panting, and then the sound of the pick at work, the dull, muffled thuds making the turf vibrate underfoot.

"Well, that's got us started," said John, turning to find Lightning and Andrew locked in a wrestling match, a trial of strength. George approached and plucked them apart like two small dogs. "Save your energy," he growled. "You'll need it before the day is over."

4.

A REVIVAL EXPEDITION

THEY NEEDED it sooner than that, however. No sooner had they been separated than the sound of voices was heard from the direction of the rock in the middle of the scrubland. The four boys stood silent, looking at each other in alarm.

"That's him," said George, nodding his head gloomily.

"Alan Hobbs?" whispered John.

"Who's he?" said Andrew, only to be ignored.

The bracken swished. There must be several people approaching. The voices ceased, then broke out again, much nearer. A moment passed, and Alan Hobbs turned the corner beside the tree. He was followed by two other boys, one a heavy character with a bullet head, the other almost as thin as George Reynolds, with a narrow face and foxy eyes.

Everybody stood still, waiting. The only sound was the rustle of bracken leaves in the breeze, and the regular thud, thud, of the pickaxe below ground.

John stepped forward. "Hallo, Alan," he said, with a friendly lift of his hand. "It's good to meet again. Are these new members of the Tomahawk Club?"

Hobbs colored, frowned, then sneered. "All that stuff?" he said. "You're living in the past. I forget your name, but I remember you were one of my team last year. I've changed things since then. What are you lot doing here, in the back of the caves? The job now is at the other end, by the river mouth where I brought you out safely."

John heard this, and looked at Reynolds. He felt anger rising and threatening to upset his grip on the situation. George stood there, looking down at a stone which he was working loose with the toe of his shoe; nobody could tell what he was thinking.

"It looks as though my memory is better than yours," said John, approaching Hobbs. The sunlight flashed on his glasses, and thus his anger would have been hidden but for the tremor in his voice and the way his head was thrust forward. "You've forgotten my name; but I remember yours. And I remember what happened last year in the cave, and out beyond it too. I remember everything, Hobbs, though I was ready to forget it if you had been friendly."

Hobbs was a much bigger fellow than he had been a year ago. And he was assured of the support of his two companions, even the weedy one with the foxy face, who had stepped behind the bullet-headed buddy when he saw John Walters' determined approach.

The reply appeared to have stung Alan Hobbs. His face grew red with rage; his mouth opened and shut several times, at a loss for words. He clenched his fist and stepped out to meet Walters. They glared at each other, two paces apart.

"What are you doing here, anyway? Why don't you stay where you belong? Isn't it good enough where you live? Let me tell you, I've got this game taped. What exploring is to be done here is being done by me and my party. So the sooner you clear out the better."

Bullet-head now stood beside him, grinning and showing a crooked tooth like a dog's fang. He twitched his broad shoulders to ease them inside his jacket.

"That's right," he grunted. Foxy wrinkled a long nose and snickered, throwing his head back so that John saw his Adam's apple wobble.

"And what do you propose to do if the Tomahawk Club carries on?"

John spoke quietly now. He had commanded the first wave of anger and was able to take stock of all three opponents: Hobbs, venomous still; Bullet-head, with that dangerous grin; Foxy, ready to make a flank attack, or to strike from behind.

Hobbs did not reply immediately. The parties faced each other, while George Reynolds slowly moved up to stand between Walters and a possible attack from Foxy. Lightning followed him, after pushing young Andrew aside.

Silence, except for the murmur of the breeze in the bracken and the steady thud, thud of Meaty's pick below ground, like the ticking of a mighty subterranean clock, in the lair of Old Father Time.

It was Bullet-head who broke the silence. "You brats want a beating?" he asked.

But the threat lost its force as his breaking voice suddenly switched from a roar to a thin piping on the last word. He looked menacing enough, however, swinging his arms lazily from those huge shoulders, and leaning forward as though to push the air aside in his willingness to hurt something.

The situation was so tense that nobody noticed how Andrew had crept into the entrance to the cave, perhaps to seek shelter.

The thudding went on underground. Still Hobbs did nothing, though he glared at Walters fiercely. Foxy edged farther to the side, intent on a loose stake which he saw as a useful weapon. It had a nasty twist of barbed wire round its blunt end. It had once been part of a fence along the edge of the wood that ran alongside the open land where now the bracken waved.

Reynolds watched him. He was uneasy, but not because of that threat—a coward's threat. He was waiting for Hobbs to say something about family matters and the change of home. Sure enough, it came.

Hobbs' expression changed. The rage against Walters gave place to a sneer, as he turned his attention to Reynolds.

"I suppose you're doing that out of gratitude to the Walters family?" A remark which showed that he had not, after all, forgotten John's name.

Reynolds flinched. Then he stepped forward, his fist clenched, having handed his stick to Lightning, who was close behind him.

This bold advance, however, did not suggest anger. It merely made Reynolds look more sorrowful, more bowed down by extreme old age, though in fact he was only a few months senior to John Walters. Yet that combination of coolness and determined purpose must have struck Alan Hobbs as being more dangerous than hot anger. He looked as though he would willingly have recalled the words which had stung Reynolds. He took a step backwards and glanced quickly to right and left. Even so, he contrived to give this hesitation an air of authority. He might have been a general summoning his troops.

Bullet-head took it so, for he shook his shoulders and stepped forward to meet Reynolds. Foxy picked up the barbed stake, stooping and remaining thus, with the stake along the ground half hidden in the undergrowth.

Lightning Soames, the quick-eyed, saw this, and jumped aside, putting himself at an angle between Foxy and Reynolds. He was watching the frontal approach of Bullet-head too, his glance darting from one danger spot to the other, wild with excitement and utterly fearless.

The battle was set. Hobbs instantly recovered, and began to threaten Reynolds alongside Bullet-head, who took another step forward, raising his red fists and laughing aloud. The dog's tooth shone like a saber in front of his face.

John Walters was handicapped by his glasses, but he had to take that risk. He knew that if he shoved them into a pocket they were just as likely to be bent or broken in a fight. Without them, too, he was so short-sighted that he was practically useless. So he had to face having them smashed into his eyes—a desperate thought to which, however, he was accustomed. In a way, this strengthened his courage.

Further, he had taken Alan Hobbs' meaning and resented the caddishness of it. He had thus two reasons for wanting to punish this handsome and patronizing fellow.

"Get out, you locals!"

It was a trumpet blast from Bullet-head, his war cry.

He leapt at Reynolds, trusting in his weight to bring the thin, lanky figure down. At the same instant, Hobbs aimed a blow at Walters with his open hand, intending to sweep off his glasses, while Foxy raised himself and drew back his arm in preparation for throwing the stake should Reynolds still be left standing after the thunderbolt of Bullet-head.

And Reynolds *was* left standing. A slow-moving mortal, he showed himself again to be quick in an emergency (as he had done last year during the crisis in the cave). He jumped to the right on one foot, and with the other tripped Bullet-head, who sprawled forward on his face. This action gave Foxy an opening, for Reynolds had moved toward him. He raised the stake; but before he could launch it, Lightning darted forward, and cut him across the elbow with Reynolds' stick. That was the first and only blow of the battle.

Foxy howled like a dog, dropped the stake, and turned on Lightning—who was no longer there. He had danced away like a sunbeam, and was menacing Foxy from behind the enemy lines, leaping up and down and laughing with delight.

The cry from Foxy had made Hobbs muff his aim at Walters' face, and this worthy seized the hand in his own and gave it a twist that sent Hobbs staggering aside, quickly to recover and prepare for a close-fisted second blow at Walters' head.

At that moment, however, there came a diversion from the rear. Little Andrew had not plunged into the mouth of the cave to hide. He had gone for reinforcements. Out he backed now, dragging Meaty by the edge of his pants, stretching them out almost to the giant's heels.

Seeing Hobbs (whom he did not love) about to overreach Walters from the side, a vulnerable point for a man with glasses, Meaty shouted and jumped simultaneously. This was quick work, for a second earlier he had been clambering out backwards from the cave, encumbered by Andrew. But hearing at once the sound of battle, he bounced his great body like a ball, as though he were an acrobat, and rolling and rising at the same time, took that leap at Hobbs which killed the blow at Walters and brought the opponent down into a clump of nettles at the wood's edge.

Rebounding from this first assault, Meaty turned, his huge, sweating face alight with good nature, and after a couple of bounds alighted on top of the rising Bullet-head, squashing him to the ground again, and weighting him down there.

"What's all this about?" he cried. "Who am I sitting on?"

John Walters, ignoring the grievance of Foxy—who was dancing up and down, nursing his elbow and spitting murder from a safe distance at Soames—now stepped forward to the fallen Hobbs, and helped him up out of the nettles.

"Yes," he said. "What's it all about? We didn't start this. I thought you had come to join the expedition. That's what I said as soon as you appeared."

But Hobbs was not to be won over. Every time he had anything to do with Walters and Reynolds he suffered some humiliation. It never occurred to him that this was his own fault. Indeed, that only made the indignity worse, since he had to cheat himself as well as the rest of the world in order to prove that he was born to command.

He sulked, scowling at Walters and Meaty.

"Cheer up," said John. "There's no ill feeling. Why don't you join us and make a good job of it?"

Meaty had meanwhile removed his massive body from that of Bullet-head, picked him up, and begun to brush the bits of crushed bracken and grass from his clothes. Bullet-head at first resented this, and raised his fist against the stranger who had treated him so roughly. But the good-natured assistance now being given took the sting out of his blow. Meaty seized the descending fist and shook it warmly, "That's right," he said. "Call it a day, and now come along with us."

Bullet-head grinned again, and the protruding tooth looked less venomous.

He was in the minority. Neither Foxy nor Hobbs could bring himself to forgive and forget. Their attention was centered on Lightning Soames, who still capered in the background, ready to come or go, crying mischief as he brandished Reynolds' stick aloft with one hand and sweeping half circles before his feet, with his own stick in the other.

"Pipe down," said Reynolds quietly, approaching and taking the first stick from him. "We want to get on with the exploring. This squabbling is a bore."

Reynolds' statement, delivered so soberly, acted as a cooler. There was a pause. Then Walters spoke again.

"What d'you say, Hobbs? Are you three coming through the caves with us?"

"No, we're not. It's the wrong tactics," said Hobbs. "That's where you need leadership. The skull was at the other end, where we came out. I've thought out a plan of campaign which will bring us to that exit where we left the caves last year. I and my team are going round by water in my father's motor launch. You lot can do as you like, but if there's anything to be found, it's the party which gets there first—well, you see what I mean. I'm fair enough, aren't I?"

Nobody could deny that, though the still fiery Lightning was heard to murmur, in derision, "I and my team!"

"I don't mind telling you," added Hobbs, now safely remounted on his high horse, "that's why we came to warn you. So now you know."

"Yes, now we know," said John. "And as we have

43

the longer job, we'll make a start. Good luck to you!"

He turned away toward the mouth of the cave, and was followed by his brother and the three members of last year's party.

Hobbs watched them, a sneer spoiling his good looks. Then he nodded to his team, as he had called them, and they fell in behind him, disappearing around the ash tree and the rock by the wood's edge.

"That's not the end of it," said Lightning. "Nothing will pull that peacock off his perch. *I and my team!* Oh yes, and my father's motor launch!"

"Well, that's right enough," said George. "It sleeps in our old boathouse, now they live next door."

John noticed that odd point of view—George calling his former home "next door," as though it meant nothing to him. It occurred to him that the quiet fellow must have suffered a lot to be able to cut away from the past like that.

These meditations were cut short by Meaty Sanders.

"Well? What about it? I don't mind telling you that I'm ravenous after all this. Jolly heavy work with that trenching tool. I must have lost about fifteen pounds in weight." He examined his huge frame ruefully. "Yes, time for a bite of something."

"But what about Hobbs and his team?" asked John. "We don't want them there first."

"Don't worry," said Meaty, handing out cheese sand-

44

wiches from his haversack. "They can't get a boat around until tonight, because of the tide. Our little river is silted up badly . . . hasn't been dredged for years, and at ebb tide the sandbank cuts off the marshy ground, all that big patch of reeds lying in front of the cliff, and the end of hills where we came out of the tunnel. Tweet! Tweet! Come on, ducky. Come on, little gell."

The last part of this was directed at a robin who, attracted by crumbs fired from Meaty's rapidly working jaws, had perched close to him and was pleading with a beady eye and a head cocked cheekily to one side. Meaty threw her a fragment torn from the sandwich in his hand just as Andrew raised a stone to throw at the bird. The robin snatched the bounty, and was away with it to a safe branch in an oak tree. Meaty, red with rage, seized the arm of the small boy, and glared at him.

"Urrcha! You killer! If you're going to be friends with me, you'll leave birds alone! Don't forget it! And a robin too! Don't you know anything? Don't you know the robin is a holy bird, and that it's terrible to kill one? Ill luck all your life. Lord! You put me off my food! Don't do it! Don't do it!"

This was a lesson for Andrew. He'd never been treated quite so fiercely, for John's control over him was a gentle monitorship, a kind of official elder-brother authority. And also, Andrew was prepared to worship

45

this huge, good-natured giant. He looked abashed, his lips trembled, and he might have disgraced himself by weeping had not Meaty instantly thrust a sandwich into the offending hand and added, "Here! Fill up with that and forget it. Only don't forget it: remember it!"—this with a broad smile that made the sun shine again for Andrew.

"He's quite right," said George, everybody having ignored this interlude—partly perhaps from a sense of guilt in the matter of stoning birds, partly to avoid making the repoof too crushing for poor Andrew, who had acted more from instinct than from cruelty.

"But there's another thing," George continued, to the sound of five sets of jaws steadily munching. "That motor launch is flat-bottomed and can creep into very shallow water."

"It can't nose its way through rushes and a mass of waterweed. The screw would foul up in a second."

Meaty refused to be hurried or ruffled. He plunged again into the haversack and drew out a jam tart.

"Ah! Don't tell me!" he said, though nobody was telling him anything. The other four boys were fascinated, watching the contest between hunger and supply.

"The trouble is," he went on, his words smeared with jam, "I can't find space enough to swing that tool down there."

He nodded toward the cave and spouted a fresh supply of crumbs, so that the robin flew down again, supported by a mate with a very dingy breast. This happy pair flickered about Meaty while he spoke, and Andrew carefully kept his gaze averted from them. He didn't want to remind himself of his recent mistake.

"We've got all day for it," said Meaty.

"Those fellows are bogged down till nearly sunset. What we want is a pinch of explosive. See what I mean? I'll go down at lunch time to my brother at the quarry and get him to give me one of the small charges. We put that in the little tunnel, and Bob's your uncle!" He beamed, and the last of the tart disappeared.

George looked solemn. "Rather risky, isn't it?"

"It'll make a devil of a noise," said John, who shared George's misgiving.

"Fine!" shouted Lightning. "Blow them to blazes! Hurray!"

He was so excited that he seized Andrew, dragged him away from Meaty's side, and began a war dance.

"Pipe down! You'll fetch the town out," said George. "But the noise might not be much, buried down there. It's a good twelve feet in, eh John?"

"I suppose so. And if we clear that passage a bit, what then? Won't it expose the entrance, make it too public?"

"No," said Meaty. "I've knocked away enough stuff to be able to pile it loose on this side of the charge.

47

That'll protect the entrance. The blast will go inward to the cave and that tight bit at the end of the tunnel where it opens down to the ledge. Look! We'll do this after tea, and tomorrow morning we'll get going through the caves. We can't start now, for we need the ropes. It's not safe, I remember, to go over that patch of shale without being roped. You've not forgotten that, Lightning? We nearly lost you that time! Well, everybody agreed?"

John and George had to fall in with this plan, though they *were* nervous.

"I suppose it's *legal?*" said John.

Everybody laughed. He laughed too, and after that the party moved off through the bracken, leaving the robins to tidy up.

5.

OPENING UP

THE BOYS met again at the Rock after tea. It
was a gusty summer evening, with rain threatening. The
wind grew rougher, blowing up the river as the ebb
tide turned. The woods moaned and the scrubland
hissed, every reed in the marshes and every frond of
bracken on the open common offering resistance to the
wind, like the strings of an aeolian harp. The whole
world twanged, and the boys realized that they were
lucky, for the sound of their explosion was not likely
to be noticed in a universe humming, scraping, moaning,
buzzing about every human ear, especially in the town
where shop blinds, gutters, street corners were adding
their notes to the symphony that grew louder and
louder as the wind strengthened.

The Tomahawks battled their way through the
writhing bracken.

"Here, take this!" said Meaty to George, handing him
a small canister about the size of a tin of bully beef. "I'll

give young Andrew a lift. It's got the devil in it to-night!"

Whether it was the canister or the bracken that was so possessed nobody inquired, for both brain and brawn were needed to negotiate a passage through the storm-tossed greenery to the mountain ash tree.

Arrived there, Meaty put Andrew down, with a pat on his fuzzy head, and took the canister from George. He produced a length of fuse from his pocket.

"That'll about fix it!"

John stood by, studying him. He compared the Meaty of a year ago, rather a fat booby, with this character, now nearly a man, practical and untroubled, somebody to be relied on for getting the odd jobs done; not quite the same as Reynolds, who also inspired confidence, but in a more remote way.

"I left the pick down there," said Meaty. "Stand by now. I'm going in!"

He stripped off his coat and sweater and, parting the bushes in front of the entrance, disappeared. Ten min-utes later he emerged, a damp smear of limestone across his hair and face. "Quick, into the wood, in case I've not covered the blast back to the entrance!"

They scrambled after Lightning, George coming last, and stood together in the green darkness of the wood, protected by the tree trunks, ashes and massive oaks.

Nothing happened, and Lightning's attention turned to the interior of the wood.

"What's that deep dip farther in?" he asked.

"You mean the dell?" said Meaty. "I don't know. It must be somewhere over the top of the main cave, where that great rock hung like a chandelier from the roof."

It was a pretty scene, with a tiny pond of water in the center of the dell, surrounded by a mass of willow herb, some in flower still, some already in seed, with silky skeins.

"Has it gone out?" whispered Andrew, looking up at Meaty. He took no notice.

Another moment passed, and several rabbits lolloped toward the dew pond from the farther side of the dell, where the wood began to rise toward the open hilltops. Nothing could be more peaceful. The storm raged above, fiercer than ever, making the tree tops mop and now, clashing their boughs, groaning and hissing. But in the trough of the dell all was quiet; hardly a breath across the glass of the little pond. A few wisps of fluff from the willow herb floated above the water, and a jenny wren flickered out of a bush and snapped up one of these drifting seeds in mid-air.

"See that?" whispered Meaty, the bird lover.

"I'm going to see what's happening," said Lightning. "Hanging about like this! It *must* have gone out!"

He darted off, and would have plunged recklessly into the entrance had not Reynolds leapt after him, and with the crook of his stick thrust forward, tripped him up.

He sat on the prostrate and angry figure.

"You fool!" he said. "Will you never learn to think twice before you leap?"

John went to support George Reynolds and together they hauled the protesting Lightning back to the safety of the wood.

This incident recalled Meaty from his bird watching.

"Can't understand it," he said. "That fuse ought not to go out. I left no kink in it round the bend into the tunnel. I'd better go and see."

"No!" cried John. "It's no safer for you than for Lightning. We must leave it until tomorrow. By the time we come with our gear in the morning, we shall know for certain if it's safe to enter."

This argument took place where the boys were standing in the wood, looking again toward the shallow dell. Lightning was still straining on the leash. Andrew also was restless, and showed signs of following his hero, Meaty, if that worthy should decide to risk entering the cave. John and George were in a minority—the cautious couple.

"It can't be done," said George, more gloomy than

52

ever. "John's right. We'll have to wait until the morning."

As he spoke, there was a dull rumble, hardly heard beneath the noise of the wind-maddened trees.

The boys stood like statues of stone, staring at each other.

The rumble ceased, returned, and grew into a steady roar. Then, before their eyes, the dell slowly collapsed; the pond broke like a mirror, the trees round it rocked and fell inward, the undergrowth boiled and coiled, then subsided into broken clots of green among the upturned tree roots, rocks, piles of new-turned earth, from which there rose a cloud of dust and the fragrant smell of fresh soil.

Slowly the movement subsided. Then, as the dust fell too, the boys saw several cracks and fissures in the debris.

"Thank goodness!" sighed Meaty, the first to recover.

"Why? . . . What?" stammered John.

"There she is!" Meaty shouted, pointing with a sausage-sized finger. "She's safe!"

Sure enough, the tiny wren still flickered about over the scene, searching for seeds in the cloud of silver which belatedly had risen from the beds of willow herb, to drift like smoke through the colonnade of tree trunks.

"But don't you see what's happened?" cried Lightning, who raged with impatience.

George replied, "Yes. So far as we can see, I believe that great pendant from the roof of the cave must have come down at last. You remember how it hung there, and how we had to stop Hobbs from trying to *shout* it down?"

"But what about the ledge?" said John. "We've probably blown that too! The patch of shale, where we had to rope together—that was already in its way a year ago!"

"It looks to me as though you've made a nice mess of things!" said Lightning, turning on Meaty.

"Stop it, you—you *gnat!*" said Meaty, putting an arm around his shoulders and nearly bringing him to earth beneath the weight of this massive limb.

"Well, we can't do much about it tonight," said George. "It's a good thing the wind is blowing like this, for nobody will have heard the explosion. We'll find those Roman remains yet! But it'll have to wait until tomorrow."

Reluctantly, they made their way back, past the mouth of the cave, over which the bushes still held guard, the only unusual feature being a film of whitish dust on the leaves.

6.

INTO THE CAVE AGAIN

THE STORM blew itself out during the night, and next morning John and Andrew woke soon after dawn, to see a sun-bathed world. The younger boy hopped out of bed and crept along the corridor, to open the door of George's room.

"Hallo!" said George, who was dressing. "You're up too? What about John?"

But John also appeared, sleepy and obviously worried.

"I've been thinking during the night, George. We're wasting our time. That charge must have blocked the narrow bit where Meaty got stuck. Also, the great ledge will no longer be safe. Why don't we start at the other end, like Hobbs?"

George hesitated, frowned. "Look here, John, I don't like meeting him nowadays. It's bad enough to have him live next door in—in my old home. Sooner or later there will have to be a showdown unless we can be kept apart. He never fails to say something nasty about my family —something you can't exactly put your finger on, but nasty all the same. You heard him yesterday?" He paused, struggling with feelings he could not put into words. "Well, that's about it. I'm just not going to risk butting into him and his affairs. D'you mind?"

John said nothing. He understood, and his sympathy for George overcame his scientific detachment.

"Right you are," he said at last. "We'll go the old way."

An hour later the three boys set out, equipped with the rope ladder which George had made last year, flashlights with reserve batteries, two candles each, two coils of rope, two spades, and rucksacks stuffed with half the wealth of Aunt Mary's larder.

These provisions had been agreed upon, and collected, the previous evening, under the supervision of that practical-minded aunt, and the doctor, former Alpine mountaineer.

"Look, George," were the doctor's last words, as the elders stood at the front door to see the start, "no heroics! See that everybody carries his burden, and does his own job. Got me? Remember that burned hand last year. That kind of thing won't do, except in story books. When there's a risk, *don't* take it."

George looked sheepish, but happy. He glanced up, first at the doctor, then at Aunt Mary who was tightening the straps of Andrew's rucksack, her face almost buried in the small boy's busby of hair.

"I understand," said George. And with that for farewell, the adventure began.

The sun beat down on the sea of bracken, which lay so still that it might have been cast in bronze. The heat brought out the salty tang of this useless but handsome frondage: the smell of high summer and holidays. A bevy of rooks drifted over the scene, almost too tired to lift their leaden wings.

"Phew!" groaned Meaty, from the top of the isolated rock. "It's a furnace up here. I'm having a Turkish bath, trying to reduce."

He joined the newcomers, who had found Lightning asleep in the shade with his back to the foot of the rock, and a spray of bracken over his head to ward off the flies.

The party rested for five minutes, to sort out the equipment and to cool off. Excitement was so high that nobody had a word to say. The only sound was the steady hum of insect wings and the fading protests of the rooks passing down the sky.

"Let's get going," said George, beginning to load himself.

"Make Andrew carry his own!" cried Lightning. "If he comes, he's to take his share." He had noticed that George was relieving the small boy of the second coil of rope.

As Lightning's protest was a reminder of the doc-

57

tor's parting words about the danger of being heroic on such expeditions and of taking on more responsibility than one was allotted, George gave way and settled the coil around Andrew's shoulders.

"We'll have to shed everything again to get through the opening," he said.

Andrew said nothing. He was puzzled by Lightning's dislike. He had not met unfriendliness before, and did not know the meaning of jealousy. He now tried to help Lightning load up, but was shaken off impatiently. So he retreated to join Meaty at the rear of the file, as the Tomahawk Club moved on through the bracken to the mountain ash tree and the mouth of the cave.

The bushes were still dusty from the subsidence after the explosion.

"I'd better go first," said Meaty. "I know how I left things yesterday, down there. We may be blocked, as John says. I'll see."

He ducked through the entrance, and Lightning followed him. There was a sound of scrambling, then of the blows of the trenching tool.

"He's clearing the muck," said John. "We'd better wait a minute."

That minute was hardly up before Lightning reappeared.

"It's all right. Meaty's shifting the stuff that he piled up yesterday. The explosion must have gone the other way, into the big cave. We can get through now, so come on!"

The air struck cold, after the August heat outside. George told Andrew to follow him, and John came last, flashing his light along the floor so that the others could see their footing.

The explosion had enlarged the short stretch of tunnel by cutting away at the floor, and Meaty could get through, this time, without having to strip to the skin, as he had done last year. He leaned over the mouth of the tunnel, closely pressed by the ever-eager Lightning.

"Wait now, while I look," he said, bringing his arm up and switching on his flashlight to examine the effect of the explosion in the great cave.

"The ridge is still there," he shouted.

The words rang round the vast, invisible walls, and died away slowly.

"Well, are you all ready?" he shouted again. And before the second echo returned, he was through, firmly set on the ledge, and had turned to assist Lightning.

A few moments later, the five boys stood on the ledge.

"Now let's all turn our flashlights up to the roof," said John. "I shouldn't be surprised if that great chandelier of rock has gone down. Something must have given way, to make all that row. It was like an earthquake; and just beneath the dell where the pond sank."

59

At first they could see little. Their eyes had not yet accepted the change from sunlight to cavernous darkness. Nor were the five flashlight beams working together. They went probing at random like miniature searchlights around a wartime sky. John put this right, and soon the beams were drawn together, directed toward the center of the dome, Andrew's being the last to come in. That was because he was the only one of the five boys who stood in the cave for the first time. He was naturally curious, and perhaps bewildered. He was also Andrew, a cub who liked to go his own way, at his own pace.

"Phew!"

The long-drawn whistle of amazement came from Meaty.

"Look at that!"

They looked, and nobody spoke.

The top of the vast roof of the cave had flattened, and the boys stared up as it were from inside an empty eggshell which had been cracked with a spoon. The cracks in the dome were like spokes of a wheel, converging to the huge original fissure which the explorers had seen, and shuddered at, last year.

"Look at it!" Lightning whispered. Even his cheeky soul was overawed. He pointed up to the center, where the great cleft had ended in the huge boss of rock which had appeared to be hanging like a gigantic chandelier

60

with nothing to support it. But that was as they saw it a year ago. The explosion had altered things.

The cleft had widened, like a mouth opening. The new cracks gathered from the opposing reaches of the roof, as unerring as spears thrust into the body of a bull. The bull was that mass of hanging rock, the pear-shaped, obscene form down which moisture trickled—the filtering perpetuation from the pond above ground. It was still a living monster. But it was also a dying monster. Only half of it shone flesh-colored in the light from the torches; the lower half. The rest was tilted toward the ceiling.

There it hung still, but at an angle, with a row of running drops, like a crystal beard, glittering on its underbody.

"But there's nothing holding it!" cried Meaty. "Oh gosh, boys! There's nothing holding it!"

He was so excited that he shouted, and jumped up and down, sending the beam from his light out of concert with the others.

Before he could bring it back to add its light to the rest, there was a rending sound. The boys saw the stalactite nod, as though the spears in its sides were draining it of its lifeblood—if such a cold, sluggish monster could be said to possess warm blood.

The movement was real enough. It happened again. They saw it: a deeper sagging, accompanied by an increase of the rending noise—and a moment later the whole protuberance parted from the roof.

Nobody could tell quite what followed. A roar; a terrible shaking of walls, the sound of water hissing and splashing, the rumble of minor concussions mingled and multiplied with echoes; a dying away and a distant return. Then silence. Silence.

"Oh God!" said Meaty. "A thing like that makes me hungry!"

He reached for his haversack, but his hand encountered Andrew's head, which the small boy had thrust into the protective folds of Meaty's garments.

"That's the second big change we've made in the geography of the caves," said John. "Last year we cut a way through by the first siphon. Now we've brought down the roof."

"That won't be the only touch," said George, gloomily. "I shouldn't be surprised if all that loose stuff along the ledge has gone too."

He was right, as they discovered after they had pulled themselves together and started off leftwards along the ridge, carefully roped.

It was not far to go. George, the leader, with Lightning Soames close at his heels, stopped short after five minutes slow progress.

"We've had it."

He flashed his light around, to warn the others to

62

stop: Lightning, Meaty, Andrew, and John in the rear.

"It's gone," he said, almost cheerfully; a prophet proud of his forecast.

The others could not crowd around him, for the ledge was not wide enough at that point. First one, then the next, stepped up, with careful handling of the rope, to peer past the leader. They saw where the weak part of the ledge, formerly that outward-tilted surface of shale whose treachery they had conquered by treading it in their socks, had crumbled away completely, except for little corbels here and there. A gap of some twelve feet lay between the boys and the continuation of the ridge.

"Now what?" said Lightning, ever impatient for the next step.

"There's only one thing," said George.

"What's that?"

For answer, George flashed his light down to the floor of the cave, fifty feet below. Then he turned it up to the roof, twenty feet above their heads.

"We can't walk like flies," he said, "so we must get down somehow. But how?"

Here John spoke, carefully putting his arm around Lightning and edging his way to the fore. "What's the edge like?" he asked George.

"Uncommonly like a decayed tooth," said George, who appeared to be enjoying a hopeless situation.

"Well, let's get the dentist to work on it," said John. "So long as we are certain the edge is firm, we can smooth it down, hang the rope ladder, and pay out the rope over it, as we did last year when Lightning and I went down the pothole to the stream. I doubt if the drop here is as deep as that. Don't you remember how much lower the floor of the river cave was?"

"And still is," said George. "Things don't change overnight in places like this."

Then everybody else laughed.

"What about last night?" said Andrew, the innocent.

And they laughed again.

"I mean acts of God," said George, still solemn. Nobody knew what he meant, and nobody cared, for attention now turned to the next stage, the immediate problem.

Meaty brought his trenching tool into play, knocking away the thin and broken rubbish from the lip of the ridge. Then he rubbed the firm edge smooth with the side of his tool, and slung the rope ladder over it, while George knocked the two cold chisels (part of the equipment of the first expedition) firmly into the angle where the ridge joined the wall of the cave.

John meanwhile, with the help of his brother and Lightning, examined by flashlight the floor below. Not much could be distinguished. Behind them glimmered the pool, where now the fallen stalactite lay half sunken, like a wallowing hippopotamus, all its majesty and life vanished. The boys could see no gap in the roof whence the rock had been wrenched. It might have been sunk in the pool for a million years.

"Ready now!" said Meaty. "But what about a bite of something before we venture down?"

"And what about it, if we get down and can't get out?" said George.

"Somebody had better make a reconnaissance," said John. "Why don't Lightning and I go, as we did last year? We know how to work together."

"There *might* be a way through," said George, who was trying to think out the plan of the caves and their connection with each other. "After all, there was that second tunnel, to the right, turning off from the last one leading out by the estuary, which we followed when Hobbs funked the plunge through the second siphon. That surely must lead into this main cave. We could go back along it, to the spot where we found the skull— which is our main object after all. That's where we want to dig."

"Listen to old Euclid," cried Lightning.

"Q.E.D."

"Good. Then let you and me prove it!" cried John.

"I want to come!" said Andrew.

65

"Yes, you would," snapped Lightning.

"Shut up, you!" said Meaty. "But what does George say?"

It was odd how George always was the member who had to give a decision when a dispute arose.

"Stick to John's plan," he said quietly. "We must wait on what they find, for it may mean that we shall have to haul them up again. If that tunnel doesn't join this cave we'll need to start again, as Hobbs said, attacking from the river entrance, by the marshes."

7.

AN INTRUDER

THE BOYS knew the technique of dropping by rope. John went first, as he had done last year down the much deeper pothole in the adjoining cave. This time he took care not to let himself start turning, like a joint of meat on a spit. He was helped because the wall had a slight tilt toward the base, and he could work his way downward with his feet touching it. A fifty-foot drop, in no confined space, is not too grim, even by flashlight.

"All set?" came George's hoarse voice from the ledge, when John and Lightning had gathered themselves together at the bottom.

"No, we've got no tools," said John. "And we'd better have one of the haversacks of food, in case we get separated from you."

The rope went up, and was lowered again, with one of the small spades and a haversack.

From the floor the cave looked double the size. The reconnaissance party felt very small as they stared up at the roof, seventy feet above. They stood close to the edge of the pond, which at this spot thrust out an arm, almost to reach the wall. The fallen monster in the middle loomed up, as big as an elephant. John shone his light on it, and saw the moisture gleaming on its colored flanks. The drip from the cracked roof fell directly on it, and at each drop it appeared to shudder in agony: a mere trick of light and water, but horrible to see.

"Ugh! It gives me the creeps," whispered Lightning. "Let's get along."

They had stood gazing at this for so long that a voice from above called, "What's up? Anything wrong?"

"No, just thinking things out," said John, a remark greeted by laughter that echoed around the cave. He might have been addressing a mass meeting.

"Well, get a move on! It'll soon be time for lunch!"

They knew whose voice that was!

It was not so easy, however, for the floor of the cave was strewn with fallen boulders and splinters of rock, the spaces between them thick with loose shale that crackled treacherously underfoot.

"Go easy now," said John, grabbing at Lightning's coat, for the small figure had darted forward. "We don't know what faces us."

Lightning waited, and as John joined him, spoke fiercely. "Why'd'you bring that kid? Far too small for this kind of job!"

68

John did not reply immediately. Nor did he point out that Andrew was much the same size as Lightning, though two years younger. Size was evidently an increasingly sore point with Lightning as time passed and he found other fellows of his own age beginning to tower above him.

"It's a strange place," he said at last. "Andrew's never visited here before, and who would he have to go with if we left him out? Have a heart, Lightning."

"Pooh! If you had a troop of sisters like I've got, you'd have hardened up long ago. Are they tough!"

This family conversation stopped as the two boys struggled over the uneven floor, hugging the left-hand wall beneath the ledge. They scrambled over the loose heap where the shale had come down from the new gap.

"That tunnel ought to come in some way along. It would be well past the point where the big flaw breaks through the wall up above."

"Unless it has some connection with it," said Lightning," and turns back from the farther cave where the second siphon makes the outlet."

"Yes. And there should be three outlets in all: the siphon, the tunnel up past the skull, and a possible one at the other end of this main cave. But I see no sign of light. It looks as though the whole thing is closed in. I had no idea it was so long. We'd better try to find that outlet first, then work our way back to this wall again.

It looks to me as though the cave bends around to the right. We may not be able to see it all from here."

They left the shelter of the wall, and thus saw the great buttress sticking out into the cave.

"That's where George burned his hand on the old oil lamp," said John, pointing up with his flashlight. From below, the great nose of rock looked formidable.

"Think of it! We all climbed over that! What a smash it would have been!" Lightning spoke as though he regretted there having been no such drama.

The voices of the rest of the party, up on the ledge, grew fainter. Three larger rocks, forming a screen, finally cut off the sound altogether.

"It still goes on," said John, after some minutes of silent progress. "And it's as I thought. The cave turns to the right, away from the other one. We must have come out between the two, through a kind of closed-in fissure."

"No, you mean the other way around," said Lightning. "It would be a boring through a wall of rock between the caves."

"Maybe," grunted John, breathless with jumping from foothold to foothold on small rocks, where the loose shale was an inch or two under water.

"Rather grim here," one of them said.

Both might have uttered that thought, for there

70

loomed ahead a blank curve where the cave closed in overhead.

"No! Look! That's *not* the end," whispered John excitedly. He flashed his light to the right. "There's a gap! We may find something round that bend!"

They did. Picking their way carefully over the water-logged surface, they reached dry ground just at the angle where the vast spaces of the main cave shrank to a kind of appendix in the far corner. Here again the water reappeared, and the boys could no longer go dryshod. They waded up to their ankles as they explored around the bend. The walls came close, leaving only a space of about fifteen feet; and the ceiling sloped rapidly, bringing the dimensions of this adjunct to the cave down to those of a room in a house.

"That's a bit more human," said John.

"You're a funny card," said Lightning. "But I still wish you'd left that kid behind."

"Oh, drop it!" said John, exasperated, as he had just stubbed his toe violently on a large stone under water. "There are some things you *have* to do."

Suddenly Lightning forgot his grievance. He had seen daylight.

"Look! There it is, John!" he cried, starting forward.

John caught up with him, and together they saw the patch of daylight veiled by a shifting net of green stuff that flickered in the open air and sunlight, blue-green and metallic, yet shot with shadows.

"We're right!" said John. "That's the third, and probably the easiest way out."

"Or *in*," said Lightning dryly. "Makes it a bit too easy for *my* liking."

They reached the opening, and found that it gave access to the world at a spot where an arm from the mouth of the river ran inland, to form a hidden stage and landing place.

It took the boys a minute or two to accustom their eyes to the glare of sunlight. They stood blinking like owls, side by side, in front of the exit.

At last they were able to survey the position roughly. The landing stage was merely a tongue of dry ground, a gravelly stretch jutting out between the river and the marshy ground which lay around the end of the hills where they came down to the estuary. It was across this marshland, where it rose to dry ground, that the explorers last year had come out of the caves. John and Lightning, turning to the west, recognized the small promontory and the group of trees and elder bushes that screened the other exit.

"That's where we came out," said John. "It's not far across, but I doubt if we can get to it from here across these reeds. They'll be under water. The river must make a great backward curve, turning east and north before it joins the Channel. What an odd bit of country! I suppose it's due to the formation of the hills, and the nature of the rocks composing them."

"What interests me," said Lightning, "is that Hobbs's motor launch is moored almost out of sight under the bank. No wonder we've missed it. Look, they've disguised it with branches of elder bush."

There it was. Lightning's quick eye had detected a gleam of white paint, the prow of the lovely creature turning eagerly out to sea under the caress of the tide, almost at right angles to the land.

"Like Hobbs!" said John. "He takes pains to camouflage the boat, but neglects to moor it fore and aft!"

"What would his old man say if it dragged away and drifted!" said Lightning. "Oh my, d'you remember the stew there was when Hobbs lost his father's famous electric lamp—how he knelt down outside the caves there and cried with fright?"

John did not reply. He was puzzled. "Look here, Lightning, I don't believe they have found this other entrance. D'you notice how hidden it is, even from us, who've just come out of it? These elder bushes grow right in front of it, and all that fern and bracken stuff makes a screen too."

"Rubbish! If their boat's here, then they must be around somewhere."

"But we know they are not in the main cave. So they *can't* have found this entrance, or entered this way."

The boys approached the launch.

"You're sure it's the Hobbses'?" asked John.

"Of course I am. There's the name, which we hear about every time we meet Hobbs in the town: the *Speed Queen*. No forgetting that!"

"But look, Lightning—in the mud patch here where the tide is falling. There's a whole lot of footprints, and men's too! Some of these are boys', but see here . . . one—two—no, three distinctly different prints of men's shoes."

"Well, Hobbs must have brought some experts along, people his father knows in the archeological world. According to Hobbs his father knows everybody at the top."

"Stop stinging! You're like a vicious little mosquito!"

Lightning ignored this criticism. He was tracing the muddy marks up and across the gravel strip, back past the mouth of the cave, and along the only stretch of dry ground beyond.

"You see, Walters? Here they go. Whoever it is, they've missed this way in. I'm not surprised, for it's down in a dip behind the bushes. Shall we trace the—?"

"No! Don't forget our party is waiting on the ledge for us to return. We can't keep them there too long.

We might go and fetch them, and come back to explore. I don't understand how this party from the launch has got across to the other entrance. There must be a dry path along the top here, where the ground begins to rise toward the bluff round the curve of the river. They *must* have gone in that way, and—"

"Down!" whispered Lightning. "Quick! Lie flat, and crawl to cover. There's someone just come in sight on that very place!"

He pulled his companion down beside him, and under the shelter of the tongue of land they edged their way toward the bushes and the hidden entrance. While thus engaged, however, they were able to see the figure of a man who had appeared suddenly from the distant group of bushes hiding the other exit. He stood looking out across the marsh, shading his eyes with his hand.

John saw a flash of light on that hand.

"I've seen that man before," he said, frowning in the effort to combat the fierce sunlight. "Yes! I've got it! He's the character who spoke to me and Andrew in the train coming down from London. Offered me a cigarette, and sneered at me when I refused it. Talked a lot, too. What on earth is *he* doing here? A very towny type, I should have thought."

While he was speaking, the stranger lifted a pair of binoculars to his eyes and began to quarter the open estuary, as though searching or watching.

75

"What's going on?" whispered Lightning. "That doesn't look like archeology."

"No, we'd better make ourselves scarce," said John. "I shouldn't want to meet that man again in a lonely place like this."

"But he must have come out of the cave," said Lightning.

"Oh Lord! Then we'll get back, as quickly as possible!"

8.

SEPARATED

ONCE INSIDE the cave again, the two boys quickly made their way back to the farther interior of the big cave and the rest of the party. They reached the wall very tired, after the scramble over the loose surface and through the waterlogged patches.

"Any news?" said George, from above.

A council was held, and after much argument it was decided that the exploration might safely be continued along the base of the wall, to seek for that possible junction with the left-hand passage leading from the farther cave, through which the river ran before passing under the second siphon and turning north into the estuary, to create the backwater where Walters and Soames had emerged to find the launch.

"So long as we know there's a second exit, we're justified in cutting off our retreat along the ledge," said George.

This conference had been held between the two boys

77

on the floor of the cave, and the three on the ledge. Thus it set up a symphony of ringing echoes.

"We're making too much noise," said George. "If John's right, and that unsavory character is prying about in the caves, we'd better sing small."

"Sing small—mall!" came mumbling back as hard and clear as a fives ball rebounding.

"What's that?" whispered John suddenly, breaking into the last coil of the echo.

"It's our voices," said Lightning. "You fussy old woman, can't you—"

"Shut up! Listen!"

Far away, somewhere yet nowhere, hollow and faint, a cry rose, then stopped with a gurgle, as though the throat uttering it had been seized.

John Walters instantly thought of the man with the flashy ring and the pointed shoes. His heart beat loudly; he could feel it, and he knew he was afraid. But he said nothing.

"Somebody in trouble," said George, quietly. "We'd better get going."

"Yes, but where?" asked John. "It came from all sides. It sounded to me as though it was near the pot-hole, along where the ledge goes into the flaw leading to the top of the hole."

"No; from up here it seemed to come right along the cave," said George. "We'll join you, at any rate, for nothing can be done from here now the ledge has crumbled away."

This was agreed, and the Tadpole was lowered, followed by the rucksacks and tools. Meaty Sanders came down last, to release the rope.

"That's two cold chisels left up there," he said. "We'll have to pick them up another day. It looks as though we've done with ropes for this journey."

"Maybe, but we'll take them along," said George, "the day's still young."

"And so is my appetite. I'm nearly starving," said Meaty. "If we're in for trouble, there's nothing like a bite of something to feed your courage."

He was already opening his rucksack when another distant sound arrested his hungry hand. By the gleam of flashlights the five boys stared inquiringly at each other.

The noise was soft, scuffling. It rubbed through the cave like the sighing of a breeze in distant woods. Then it died away.

"You know what that means?" said George, after a long silence. "It must have come through an opening along this wall. Whatever is going on is taking place in the river cave or the tunnel leading from it into this one —the tunnel we left unexplored."

"Hitch up!" ordered Meaty, the words distorted by a sandwich crammed hastily into his mouth.

No further sounds reached the Tomahawk Club, though its members moved close to the wall where the floor was free of loose shale, being overhung by the projecting wall of the cave. George led the way, with Lightning, John, Andrew, and Meaty.

"Quietly now," came the order from George, who since the shock of that distant cry of distress had naturally taken command of the expedition.

It was not so easy, however, to move without a sound over the floor, for though it was firm under the wall it was not level, and it was also occasionally obstructed by a bit of rock or a cleft, unrevealed by torchlight— traps for the feet of the explorers. John turned to make sure that Andrew was making the pace comfortably. In turning, he brought the spade, carried shoulder-arms, with a smack against the wall. Everybody stopped.

"Sorry," whispered John.

"Yes. We're getting near the spot surely," said George, also whispering. "That tunnel must come out along here soon."

They passed around the place where the ledge swelled out to make a broad platform. It towered over them as a vast canopy, without a break or any sign of a flaw to match the break above the platform that led through to the pothole.

Lights were flashed upward, but the projection hid everything.

"Don't you think the sound may have come through the second flaw that led you, Meaty and Hobbs into the roof of the river cave?"

"Maybe. But I've a hunch that we might have heard nothing if there weren't more than one contact. Let's go on."

George started off as he replied, and the others followed dutifully.

They reached the buttress, that stood out from the wall as a muscular bastion towering up for fifty feet. The boys were forced to creep around it, encountering the loose shale of the mid-floor.

"Go slow; lift your feet high and don't shuffle through this stuff!"

Everybody obeyed George's whispered order, and the quiet progress was maintained, bringing the boys back to firm footing beyond the buttress or pilaster, deep into the bay beneath the ledge.

Flashing their lights upward again, the boys saw across the bay the dark flaw that rose for fifty feet, through to the river cave and the slope with the fifteen-foot drop down the wall to the place where the river flowed under the first siphon. That was the scene of last year's labor when the Tomahawk Club, working on both sides of the rock partition above the siphon, broke it down, to enable John and Lightning to rejoin the rest of the party.

"We must be getting near," said George. "As quiet as you can."

His warning was timely. A distant, but not-so-distant, laugh came through the echo chamber, faint, hollow. It was evil.

"That's a man," said Lightning. "It can't be Hobbs' party."

George said no more. He had already moved forward and was lost in the dim and threatening shadows gathered around the tiny group.

"Keep up with him!" whispered John. "We don't know what lies ahead." But Lightning had already darted forward, and was at George's heels. The two disks of light flickered around the wall of the cave like the ghosts of silver coins.

Suddenly the two tiny searchlights drew together and settled.

"Come along," Meaty breathed through his fragrant mouthful of sandwich. "They've stopped! They've found something!"

George was peering up at a small opening in the wall, about the size and shape of a porthole.

"I believe that's it. But how are we to get through? It'll just about take Lightning and Andrew, but the rest of us couldn't do it. It's rather high, too: and we don't know what the drop is on the other side. That floor may be much lower than this."

"At any rate, I'm going!" cried Lightning, his voice shrill with excitement. "That kid's too young to try it."

Andrew said nothing, but he was already dragging a flat piece of rock into position beneath the hole to make the first step. Meaty followed his example, and nobody appeared to be concerned about the practicability of struggling through the hole to unknown hazards in the darkness of the tunnel, which might, or might not, be the connection whose other end the boys had seen last year, just before finding the Roman skull.

Four bits of rock piled below the hole made a platform for one of the smaller boys to reach up. Andrew, without a word, leaped forward. He stood on the platform and was about to heave himself up when Lightning, with an exclamation of rage, seized him round the waist and dragged him down.

"He can't do it! Look here, Walters, keep your young brother in order. Suppose he—"

"Leave go! I can look after myself. Because I'm younger than you, I've been bullied ever since we started!"

"We could do without you, Tadpole! You're here on sufferance."

They would have fought had not George put a hand on the shoulders of both angry boys.

"You're behaving like kids, at any rate. Don't you realize that we need to keep quiet? We've got to find

83

out what is happening. Now, fall in! We must work together."

He emphasized his words with a friendly thump on each small back.

"You, Lightning, are the one for the job. You know the possible lay of the land. Go through, and let us know if this is a lead into that other exit. We'll wait."

John stepped quietly to his brother and murmured something that smothered any protest. Without more delay, Lightning Soames sprang onto the stones, turned and handed his gear to George, and pulled himself up to the hole.

"Don't show too much light," said George, for Lightning was flashing his light into the opening. "And don't let yourself be seen, either."

"I've got to see where I'm going," Lightning protested. "It looks clear. Much wider inside, and runs down a bit. That would be right, wouldn't it, if it's to join the other tunnel coming out of the river cave?"

George did not answer, for another muffled laugh came from the undetermined distance underground. It quietened the boys.

"There's something going on outside, too," whispered Meaty under his hand, and close to George's ear. "At the other opening."

"Quiet, then. They may come in that way. If so,

84

we'll creep in behind the great buttress. They probably won't penetrate as far as that. You'd better come down, Lightning."

But he was too late. Lightning was already halfway through the hole when the alarm was given. Another wriggle, and he disappeared. A second later, the other boys heard a heavy bump, and a groan.

John instantly leaped up and thrust his head and shoulders through the hole. Flashing a light downwards, he saw Lightning crumpled below.

"What's the matter?"

A white face gleamed.

"It's farther than it looked," Lightning murmured, obviously in pain but striving to ignore it. "I dropped and turned my ankle. And I think I've bashed my knee too." He moaned as he tried to pull himself up.

"What do we do now?"

"Wait a bit, Soames. Take it easy and don't try to move. We may have to come around the outside to get to you."

"Oh Lord, don't be long. I can't stick this alone."

John withdrew, and reported to the others.

"I'm going through to him," said Andrew, with so determined a temper that nobody attempted to stop him.

"Well," said his brother, "you know it's a long drop. And you'd better take the first-aid kit. He may have cut his knee. You know what Aunt Mary taught us!"

"And try to find a foothold down the other side of the wall. Don't jump it!"

These instructions from John and Reynolds fortified the Tadpole. He thrust the kit importantly into his hip pocket, tightened his belt, and with Meaty's aid reached up to the hole. A moment's pause at the mouth of it, and he had gone. But his fingers could be seen, clinging to the edge. John jumped up at once, and whispered anxiously.

"I'm all right," said Andrew. "Coming, Lightning! There's plenty of grip down the wall."

"For Heaven's sake keep quiet, both of you," said John, thinking suddenly of that unpleasant character whom he had last seen driving past in the tumble-down sports car, with two other roughnecks.

He saw the Tadpole creeping down the ten or twelve feet like a small beetle. The boy reached bottom safely, landing beside the twisted figure of Lightning.

"Can you walk if I help you?" Tadpole asked.

Lightning tried to heave himself up, with Andrew's aid, but collapsed with an exclamation of anger and pain.

"Get out! Get back!" he said.

"No, I'm staying with you," said the Tadpole.

"Well I'm—" But Lightning did not perjure himself further, for once again sounds penetrated from the other end of the tunnel—sounds of bundling, bumping, with grunts and muffled words.

"Ssh!" whispered Andrew, as he tried to move Lightning into a comfortable sitting posture with his back to the wall.

Then, with his light close to the damaged knee, he found that it was badly grazed and bleeding.

"Hold tight, it may sting," he said, getting out the first-aid box.

"What cheek!" muttered Lightning. But it was a most friendly exclamation. "You needn't stay, you know," he added, but only half-heartedly.

The Tadpole went on bandaging and made no reply.

"You slipped through that hole easily enough," muttered Lightning, through his teeth because the pain was sharp. "I could hardly struggle through."

Andrew's fuzzy head was bent over the damaged knee, so Lightning could not learn if his remark went home.

9.

CONTRABAND

Now what do we do?"

Nobody answered John's question. He, Meaty and George stood below the hole, listening to the faint murmur of voices from the other side, and looking at each other, nonplussed.

"There's only one course," John said. "It's what I told Lightning. We must try to get round by the other opening. But that man is watching in front of it."

"We must do it, though," said George. "It's no use hanging about here. Lightning has evidently sprained his ankle, or even broken it. We've got to get him out. The Tadpole can help him meanwhile. They'll get to know each other better!"

"It's no laughing matter," said John, who was still worrying about Andrew, and the nearness of that unpleasant character whom they had met in the train.

"I'm not laughing," said George. "But I think young Tadpole can look after himself, and Lightning too. He

88

knows what he wants and goes for it without too much talk. Always a good sign, that."

"He's only eleven."

George patted John on the shoulder, "Come on; stop worrying! We'll get along again."

He loaded himself with gear, including the rope which Lightning had formerly carried. The others followed suit. John first leaped up to the hole, thrust his head through, and whispered, "Look! We're going out, to try to get round to you. Keep smiling, and don't move far. Okay?"

"Move far! I'm crippled for life!" hissed Lightning. "And now you thrust the Tadpole on me, as though I've not already enough to handle."

John felt Meaty plucking at his coat, so he said no more and jumped down, to follow where George had already made a start. He hurried forward. "I'd better lead the way."

"Carry on," said George. "Don't fuss about those two. I don't believe Lightning's as bad as I said. He's a bit of an actor, you know. Has to be, with all those sisters to contend with."

"Count me out," said Meaty. "I can't get a word in edgeways. I'll put my money on the Tadpole—young Andrew. Plucky kid. I could teach him to box, if I had him down here for a term or two. I know his kind; they never know when they're beaten, and always bob up again, like my Old Man. The old boy was in the Navy during the war, and put on so much weight that the Admiralty tried to invalid him out. So he volunteered as a stoker. He got himself down from two hundred fifty-two pounds to two hundred twenty-four in a few weeks. I believe he'd have stayed on after the war, only Mum couldn't run the butchery business alone. They're a tough lot in our trade!"

This bit of family history helped the three boys along, and they soon found themselves wading through the waterlogged shale around the bend.

At the first gleam of daylight the boys hesitated, stopped.

"Now we'd better do a bit of scouting," said George. "Look, John, you're cautious enough. Creep along a bit and have a look around outside. You know the lay of the land."

John, amused at this last remark by a native to a visitor, crept forward, carefully picking his way to avoid making a sound. He could see the sunlight on the thick screen of bracken and elder bush at the mouth of the cave. He might have been a fish looking out from an aquarium. The lights and shadows mingled with an oily smoothness, one depth of green into another, and all of them touched with golden fire.

"Keep going!" He heard the loud whisper from Meaty. It made him realize that he had stopped to admire the screen of living light in front of his eyes. Turning, he saw the two faded medals of flashlight beams, already dim against the penetrating day-fire.

There was no sound, except the murmur of summer breathing over the outside world. John approached the opening, his eyes now blinking. With added caution he stooped, pressed himself against the wall at the entrance, then went down on all fours and crawled out, slowly parting the grasses and fronds of bracken as he reconnoitered.

He was not quiet enough, however, to reassure a pair of herons standing in the sandy mud below the landing stage, examining, with the usual curiosity of all birds, two large square packages. Simultaneously, the herons turned their heads toward John, dropped a suspended leg, spread their pinions, and after a preliminary beat, rose superbly into the sky and oared away toward the open Channel.

This graceful little drama was ignored by John. He had seen the packages. With a low whistle, he backed into the cave, to find George and Meaty waiting just inside.

"Somebody's been here since Lightning and I came!"

"How d'you know?"

"There are two big parcels dumped on the landing stage. And—but listen; that's the sound of a motor boat!"

91

It was very faint, dying away. Then it ceased.

"Was the boat there too?" George asked.

"I couldn't see. The tide is falling, and the water is well below the level of the boards."

"Well, we'll explore. Come along, Meaty, we may need your fists and muscles. But you go first, John. Make for the edge, and we'll satisfy ourselves that nobody's about."

✻The cover of undergrowth favored the boys almost to the miniature and dilapidated landing stage, which was only three planks wide. The tall grass overhung its sodden boards and spilled seed on them. Bird droppings and tiny shells of snails and sea vermin decorated them with long-seasoned patterns, fingered by many weathers.

The parcels looked all the more neat and new, in contrast to the place where they stood.

"Somebody's been in a hurry, to dump them in the open just like that. Looks to me as though they've gone back for more," said George.

"Gone back where?" asked Meaty, who found his supine posture irritating. He was also itching to get at his haversack, for some time had passed since he swallowed that sandwich.

"That we don't know. But I should say it must be to a seagoing vessel lying out in the Channel."

Meaty's large frame heaved, like that of a hippopotamus rising out of a tropical swamp.

"Oh boy! You mean? Of course, it's a job of smuggling!"

"What else would it be?" asked John, craning his neck to examine the parcels. "They're square, and covered in waterproof. Well packed. Must be something valuable. Can't see any labels or names."

"Not likely, if they're what I suspect," chuckled George. "But we'd better vanish. I'm certain that boat's returning soon, with another load. They'd bring the stuff in by driblets, in case of being caught. Come on, we'll retreat and work our way unseen around the bluff to the other entrance. There's nobody there either, at the moment."

"I'll just make certain about the Hobbs launch," said John.

He crawled forward, and a moment later returned.

"Yes, it's gone. That's why it was covered with branches—they wanted to screen it. But I say—what about Hobbs and his party? They can't be concerned in this, surely?"

All three boys stared at each other. A low whistle of incredulity formed on Meaty's fleshy lips.

"Whatever it is, it serves him right," he said. George did not reply. A conflict of strong feeling made him stand there, frowning and bewildered. Suddenly he turned, shook himself, picked up his gear, and started away. The others followed, Meaty hastily grabbing the coil of rope which he had dropped, with a view to exploring his haversack again.

"Oh golly!" he groaned, swinging the rope loosely on his shoulder, with the running loop in his hand.

They moved back first to the rising ground, where rocks and scrub, with patches of tamarisk and elder, gave ample shelter. The slight elevation gave them a view over the water where the river joined the main Channel. Half a mile out stood a grimy tramp steamer. A long tanker was slowly steaming up Channel, and the boys could hear its distant chug-chug. The only other vessel in sight was the Hobbs's motor launch, with two men in it, approaching the tramp steamer lying asleep on the sun-dazzling water, a tiny thread of smoke hovering about its funnel. Gulls wove an invisible tracery around the vessel, and their cries came faintly to the boys' ears.

"That's what it looks like," said John. "Those two men would be the people who passed us on the way here, and nearly pushed us off the road."

Far up the coast, the two herons had alighted, pearl-gray dots. John saw them as he looked upstream. He did not see a black dot, farther along, slowly moving inshore, approaching the mouth of the tributary.

Step by step, keeping watchful cover, the three boys

moved westward, followed the curve inward, then rounded the bluff, to come upon a wider view down Channel toward the open sea. It was a grand sight, with the waters spreading out, the distant shores across the estuary moving up and out of sight northwestward, backed by mountains, dour even from this distance: the sleepy traffic, a collier here, a few fishing trawlers more remote, an ocean-going monster merely a ghost almost hull-down: and over-arching all, the certainty and splendor of the blazing sunshine, that blinded yet revealed. It was something solid, not only to be seen but touched, as metal, and smelled, as salt, and felt, as healing fire.

"Phew!" sighed Meaty. "Am I sweating, after those cold caves!"

"Well, we haven't done yet," said George. "Look! There's the spot where we came out last year—with the marsh in front of it; quite near now."

"Nobody about, though," said Meaty.

He had no sooner spoken than the undergrowth a little way along suddenly heaved, and a moment later there broke out of it a struggling mass.

"Quick!" cried George. But Meaty put out a hand and dragged him back.

10.

THE RIVAL PARTY

WHEN ALAN HOBBS and his two friends from boarding school, Bullet-head and Foxy, had left the members of the Tomahawk Club, they wasted no time. Early next morning they crept down to the boathouse, where the speed launch lay ready. The loading had been organized by Foxy, a clever fellow for plotting and planning. He was not one to be caught unawares. He had seen to it that the locker carried flashlights, as well as the big electric lamp, the replacement of that destroyed during last year's exploration of the caves. An extra coil of rope, a six-inch ordnance map of the few square miles of the town and the river mouth, an axe and a spade, completed the preparations which Hobbs and Bullet-head had left to Foxy.

Hobbs was so much concerned with the grand idea of *really* being leader of this new expedition, so proudly equipped, that he had no time to bother about details. As for Bullet-head, all he wanted was something to bite on: a good fight, anything that would challenge his strength.

While they were hurrying to the boathouse, Bullet-head referred to that worthy opponent, the huge fellow who had sat on him by the mountain ash tree. He spoke almost with affection.

"Tough lad, that! I'd like another go with him. I'll bet he knows the science. With that fist he ought to have a punch like an ox!"

"You mean the butcher's boy?" said Hobbs.

The sneer in his voice made Bullet-head look at him oddly. "Well, a fight's a fight," he said.

Foxy laughed. "You haven't got his meaning," he said.

"No?" Bullet-head was not so blunt as he looked. He winked at Foxy.

Hobbs was in front, and missed all this. He was intent on one thing, to get first to the place where the skull had been found. He saw fame in this adventure. He did not intend to share it with Walters and Co.

He put his thoughts into words, so eager was he. "Look! That fellow Walters is just a visitor down here, coming and going, and picking out the plums!"

"So are Foxy and I, come to that," said Bullet-head.

"Yes, but you're working for me. That makes it different."

"It's scientific, as we go about it," said Foxy.

Bullet-head couldn't follow that. His silence was so blank that it stifled the discussion. The two boys followed their leader, impressed in spite of themselves, by the lofty claim made by him.

There was neither food nor drink in the launch. Foxy could not reasonably raid the kitchen and pantry in a house where he was a guest. Hobbs had not thought it necessary to contemplate a long session in the cave. He explained why, as the launch carried them rapidly downstream, sending a giant mustache of water curling from its prow, to widen into a wake that broke the reflection from banks and sky, and nuzzled with little gurgles at the rat holes and exposed tree roots.

"We'll be there in half an hour. It won't take long to dig around that spot in the tunnel. It's only a few feet wide, and if I remember rightly—I've got a good memory—the floor is soft sand just there. We'll quarter the floor yard by yard. I've been reading it up in a book on archeology. The thing's got to be done properly, and scientifically, as I said to Jones."

Jones was Foxy. He did not think it worth while to point out that it was he and not Hobbs who had started the idea that science was to be used on the job. Hobbs had that effect on people, even after they had found him out. Bullet-head winked again at Foxy—which may have meant that he was still content to play second fiddle.

The speed launch was a living creature. It reveled in the water, like a dolphin over the waves of the tropics. The sun glittered on its tiny decked prow, and flashed on the chromium-plated vents. The boat half rose out of the water when Alan Hobbs increased speed, at the approach to the open Channel. It smacked at the wavelets, crumpling them down beneath its flat white belly.

"Oh boy!" sighed Bullet-head, staring along the boat, half in love with it. He looked too at the leader, his host, who sat handsomely at the tiller, proud, almost disdainful.

"We'll beat them by half a day," said Alan Hobbs, looking at his wrist watch. "My guv'nor doesn't know we've borrowed the *Speed Queen*. We'll have to get back before he gets home from London this afternoon." A shadow passed over his proud face, as though the sun had disappeared, and a chill wind risen. But he was quickly master of himself again, and in command of the expedition.

He certainly knew his way in home waters.

"Look, that's where the underground stream joins our river." He pointed to a break that made the bluff a double promontory. "Around now to the little stage."

The boat swirled to the right, almost on its own length, and beat back toward the shore. Alan had sailed out farther than was necessary, in order to show the paces of the launch. Its power added to his power.

99

Oddly enough, with all his knowledge of the waters of the river mouth, he knew nothing about the coast, or of the caves. He drew skillfully to the landing stage, and left Foxy to make the boat fast.

"We'll take the rope and tools," he said, whereupon Bullet-head picked up the axe and spade, while Foxy brought the coil of rope and a gardener's trug. "Let's see." Hobbs paused. "Yes, that's the place where I brought them out last year. Around the first bluff and beyond that stretch of marshy ground."

Being town boys, they did not observe that the dry ground between the marsh and the broken cliffs had recently been trodden; the bracken, grass and patches of sea lavender bent to the ground.

Rounding the bluff, they halted before a thick bank of tamarisk.

"It was somewhere around here," Hobbs said, as he disappeared behind the bush. "Come on!"

The others followed him, to find the wall of rock at an angle and broken like a harelip. Into the fissure Hobbs stooped, and led the way down the passage for some forty yards, where it leveled out and widened over a surface of loose sand.

As the tunnel curved between this level stretch and the opening, no daylight filtered through. By flashlight, which to sun-accustomed eyes was still but a feeble aid, the boys saw that the sandy surface was raked smooth.

The teeth marks of the rake made a grid pattern in the sand.

"Hm! They left it tidy last year," said Hobbs.

"Who's they?" said Foxy, suspiciously.

"Dr. Walters and the local archeological society. They came prying about after my discovery of the skull. It was they who took it away and sent it to the museum for identification. My father says they're a very amateur lot. He won't have anything to do with them. Some day, when he's got a bit of time to spare, he intends to make a really thorough search of the whole system of caves in this part of the country—do the thing on a big scale."

"Any money in it?" asked Foxy.

"You never know, we might also find buried treasure. Great country for smuggling and wrecking, in the past. These caves by the sea are the perfect hideout for games of that sort. But that's all over now."

"Sure," growled Bullet-head. "Smuggling today is done at the airports—small stuff, too; drugs and all that. No more kegs of brandy and bales of lace!"

He laughed with glee at the picture of violence which his words had conjured up.

"Well, what do we do now?" asked Foxy.

"We begin a systematic search on this very spot. It was here the skull lay half buried, I should say."

As Hobbs spoke, he began pacing out measurements,

and decided that the find had been made halfway between the walls of the tunnel.

"But wait a minute," said Foxy, stooping and examining the rake marks in the sand. "This looks to me as though it was smoothed over less than a year ago. Look, it's still damp and darker in the ridges."

"Don't be an ass," said Hobbs. "You've got a nose that smells a plot everywhere. Who on earth would be coming here after all the fuss made by the society about the public not disturbing the site?"

"I should, for one. And I bet that crowd we met this morning have already been prowling around. That lanky fellow who used to live in your house. He's not one to leave a mystery alone."

"Mystery? It's no mystery! It's a plain case of Roman remains, and all we've got to do is to get in first before that chap Walters, prompted by his uncle, arrives on the scene. He's more inquisitive than Reynolds. Why, Reynolds does nothing but moon about painting and drawing, since he went to live next door after his own mother ran off with—"

"What's that?" Bullet-head, bored by this talk, suddenly interrupted.

"What's what?" Hobbs was annoyed.

"Listen!"

"Sounds like somebody at the entrance. Yes, it's men's voices."

Foxy shivered, took a pace or two toward the distant sound, then crept back, to whisper: "We'd better not be found here, with all these tools. It would give the whole game away. What shall we do?"

"We can only retreat," said Hobbs. "Bring the stuff, and we'll go on to the cave where the river flows through."

Loading up with the tools, the three lads went on along the tunnel, which rose and fell switchback fashion, with curves to right and left following the cleft in the rock formations. From time to time they stopped, to take breath, to ease their backs (for now they were bent double under the low ceiling) and to listen.

"Are they following?" It was Foxy's frightened voice.

"No," said Bullet-head. "And what if they are? It's probably only a holiday party."

"Not so far out of the town as this," quivered Foxy. "And around all that no-man's land we crossed."

"Well, there's no sound now," said Hobbs. "If you'd only stop chattering we could make sure. Then we'll wait here until we're certain they've gone away. Time's passing, and I've got to return the launch before my Guv'nor comes home. There'd be the devil to pay!"

He was obviously worried about this matter of borrowing his father's launch without permission.

Five, ten minutes passed, and no further sound.

"I'm getting a bit peckish," whispered Bullet-head. "Could do with a couple of ham rolls! A pity we didn't bring—"

"Can't carry everything," said Hobbs irritably. "It would have given the game away if we'd raided the larder at home. Mother might have spilt to the Pater, and that would be the end."

"The end of what?" Foxy asked. He liked to get things taped. It made him feel safer. But Hobbs ignored this question.

"It's all clear. Must have been some holiday makers landed from a joy ride. They've cleared off without noticing the cave. After all, it's fairly well hidden, though they must be pretty dim-witted not to spot it, with only a few bushes to cover it. If I'd been mucking around there for the first time, I'd have pried about a bit, and found it."

"Sure," said Bullet-head. He sounded sleepy, even sulky. He was bored with hanging about, and nothing happening. Ancient history meant little to him. "What do we do now?" he demanded.

"We'll go back and make a start," said Hobbs. "It's late already. We've got an hour to prod about in that sandy floor. What I'm after is the rest of the skeleton."

They crawled back to the wider and loftier stretch of the tunnel, just before the last bend at the approach to the entrance.

"Still no sign of anybody outside?" asked Foxy, not fully reassured.

"Forget it!" growled Bullet-head. "Even if they do come back, we'll scare the pants off them," and he made a whinnying noise like the ghost of a horse.

"Keep it down," whispered Foxy. "You never know!"

Without further delay they got to work. Hobbs superintended, looking around, pointing things out, and telling his henchmen where to dig. Bullet-head handled the spade, and Foxy fiddled about with the axe, turning it flat and scooping up driblets of sand. Both boys worked, as Hobbs directed, in a circle from the central spot where he believed the skull had been found.

It was a monotonous job, but suddenly Bullet-head gave a low whistle. "Hallo! What's this?"

"Take care now!" Hobbs instantly exclaimed. "We mustn't break any of the bones. And we've got to make notes of the position. Got your notebook, Jones?"

Jones had already dropped his axe, and now he whipped out a small exercise book from his hip pocket, and stood, peering over Bullet-head's bent body, the flashlight in his left hand throwing a thwart beam along the sandy floor.

Hobbs darted in too, and all three boys stooped, with their backs to the entrance and the bend in the tunnel.

The big lantern lit up the spot where Bullet-head's spade had struck something solid.

"Now then!" cried Hobbs, his voice shrill with excitement. "Go carefully. Ease the sand off it to right and left. For Heaven's sake don't plunge the spade into it. Those bones will crumble at a touch. They're nearly two thousand years old, don't forget!"

To make sure of not injuring the Roman warrior, Bullet-head put the spade aside, knelt down, and began to part the sand with his hands. After a few moments of this rabbit-like scrabbling, he looked up, while his hands still groped in the sand.

"It's not bones at all," he said. "I believe it's something more solid. Feels like a—"

But before he could say what it felt like, he toppled into the shallow hole of his own making, with somebody on his back. At the same time both Foxy and Hobbs were seized from behind, and their flashlights snatched from them.

A grunt. Several exclamations of rage, followed by a sinister chuckle.

"Now then!" said a man's voice. "Let's tie them up, and ask a few questions!"

Before the three boys could realize what had happened, they were trussed up with the long coil of rope from the launch. Bullet-head, enraged, let out a bellow like an ox, but his still invisible assailant gave him a thump between the shoulders that made the cry die out a gurgle, as though he were being strangled.

The light of their own lantern, and Foxy's flashlight, being turned on them, the boys still failed to see beyond the glare, where their attackers stood in darkness.

"What's all this about?" said the cockney voice. "Cough it up! Who gave you the lowdown on this, eh? What are you expecting to find?"

"We're archeologists," whispered Foxy, who was shivering with fear. Bullet-head said nothing. He was already trying to test the strength and nature of the knots that bound his hands behind his back. Hobbs managed to find a voice, protesting and blustering.

"Look here, you've no right! When my father hears of this, he'll—"

"Cut that out," said the second man, behind him. "Stick to what you're being asked. What is it you're after? And who let you in on this?"

"I don't know what you're talking about," said Hobbs. "It's quite right. We're looking for the bones of a—for archeological remains!" He was still sufficiently master of himself to realize that he had nearly betrayed his mission to these strangers.

"Make him squeal!" said the cockney voice, with a nasty snarl. "We've no time for all that stuff. There's the other parcels to bring in yet before we're safe."

Hobbs hardly knew what followed. He felt himself

seized by his coat collar and half lifted off his feet. A second later, an agonizing pain shot up his arms and shoulders as the man behind him brought the loose end of the rope across his back. It caught the pinioned arms. He screamed, but a hand was clapped instantly across his mouth, making him cut his lip on his teeth. The scream died away into a frightened whimper. Nobody had touched Foxy. He was lying low, and waiting.

"Now then! Out with it. You'll get another taste o' the rope if you don't speak up."

"I tell you we're looking for a Roman soldier," whimpered Hobbs. His back burned and throbbed, and he was not quite coherent. He was ready to confess anything to avoid a second flogging. He was not even put to shame when he saw Bullet-head take a dose of the rope end, without flinching. The tough fellow just knelt there, his head sunk in his shoulders. Foxy again managed to be overlooked. That was his strongest suit; the reason, perhaps why he got along very nicely in life.

The man with the rope end was about to apply it again to the bowed backs of Hobbs and Bullet-head when the second man stopped him.

"We don't want a lot more trouble," he said. "We've got to think of things later on. These kids may be up to some other game, after all."

"Shove 'em along to the cave," said the third voice. "Time's running out, and so is the tide. So long as they don't see what our business is, not much harm will be done. We'll be finished, and cleared, before they can get away." Then he whispered to the first bully, "We'll release them when the stuff is collected. But it means we can't leave any packages here, blast their eyes! We must move it all out again."

The boys were forced, under threat of the rope end, to crawl along the tunnel—no easy matter with their arms tied behind them and the rope dangling between their legs. But urged by the impatient and fierce threats of the first man, and an occasional wild kick from his pointed shoe, they found themselves in the cave which Hobbs was just able to recognize (he was half blind with fear and rage) as the one where the stream ran through, and under the siphon to the outer world.

"Now you young blighters, this'll teach you not to poke your nose into other people's business. Just you wait there until we come back. And it won't be for some time. We've got a lot of work to do."

With that, the boys were trussed together, tied by their feet as well as their hands, uncomfortably fixed back to back, and deposited like a trice of partridges after a shoot, under the overhanging wall of the cave where the tunnel gave on to the open floor, in the direction of the steep sloping ledge down which Hobbs, Reynolds and Meaty Sanders had found their way a year earlier, in order to rejoin Walters and Lightning Soames.

But that was an old story, with some excitement to it. Things were different now, humiliating and beastly.

The men retreated. They could be heard in the tunnel, still angry, muttering to each other, the one full of threats. But the sound died away, save for a distant scuffling, and the silvery sigh of sand running off a spade.

"That's *our* spade," whispered Foxy. "They've no right to use it."

Bullet-head chuckled. He was not subdued by his ignominious position, or cowed by the sting of the rope end on his broad back.

"And they've no right to use *us* like this either," he said, turning his head in the effort to see Foxy. But their flashlights were in the possession of the men, and the only light in the cave was from the faint, green infiltration through the running stream where it slipped with tiny chuckling regularity under the siphon. Bullet-head, through this dim aid, saw Foxy still shrunk into himself like a hedgehog rolled into a ball, ready to take a peep out at a dangerous world when a chance should occur. Hobbs, to the other side of Bullet-head, was in a state of collapse. The degradation of the flogging, the pain of the bonds, the ignominy of this unexpected loss of freedom, and above all, the worry about not being able to ensure getting home with the *Speed Queen* before his father should return from London, mounted to a formidable load of misery, and he could not carry it. He hung in the ropes; and without the support of his friends, to whom he was tied, he would have fallen, completely demoralized.

"Hold up, Hobbs," whispered Bullet-head. "We're not dead yet. Don't pull on the rope like that. Ease it toward me. I'm trying to free my wrists. It feels slack, and if I can work one hand over the other, I'll manage to loosen it. Look here, Jones, can't you lean back? I'll shove my wrists under yours, so that you can fiddle with the knots."

This plan of action restored morale somewhat. Bullet-head and Foxy, ignoring Hobbs who was bemoaning his fate, worked away like mice. It was a task that would take time. These men had a professional touch in this matter of rough handling. The boys knew they were up against the real criminal world.

Meanwhile the three men had returned to the spot where the sand was spread evenly, except for the clumsy efforts of the boys.

"What's all that bluff about a Roman soldier?" said the gentleman with the pointed shoes and town suit. "I bet they saw us bring the stuff in."

"Maybe," said the one who had prevented a second flogging. He seemed to be more intelligent, and alert to the risks involved in tying up these young intruders. He was obviously worried, and anxious to remove all questionable signs. "But I've heard something about Roman remains being found here last year. These young blighters may be telling the truth. We're just unlucky, that's all. And we've got to get out of it, with no time lost."

"I've got it!" said the third man. "With that launch, we can run the stuff back in double quick time, and put it under cover while we think up another way of bringing it in. Quick, now! That's the idea! Two of us can load it up and make a couple of journeys, while one stays at the mouth of the cave here to keep a lookout along the Channel and the waterfront. We can do the whole thing in an hour, surely!"

With that, they instantly got to work, raking the sand back with the spade and uncovering several square parcels wrapped and sealed in waterproof plastic.

"Take care now! Don't jolt them," said the second man, who appeared to be the leader. "They won't take too much rough handling. Phew! I'll be mighty glad when we get them off our hands."

"Well, if it weren't for these varmints," said Pointed-shoes, "we'd have done our part when we left the stuff buried here for the Boss to collect. As it is, with all this coming and going, the Revenue men being on the prowl up and down the coast, we're as likely as not to be spotted."

"Well, you keep watch outside and give us the signal

if you see them while we are crossing to the ship. With that launch, we could turn out to sea and run for it, then double back to the hideout near the Atlantic Docks."

They were so closely occupied with this job of removing the contraband, and sneaking it down to the jetty under cover of the cliff, that they gave no more thought, for the time being, to the three boys whom they supposed to be securely pinioned in the farther cave.

Thus, none of them noticed the cautious observer in the tunnel, crouched down to the ground against the wall, just around the bend. It was Bullet-head, biding his time.

II.

BATTLE ROYAL

WHILE MEATY SANDERS dragged George Reynolds back with one hand, he thrust out his other arm as a barrier, and drew John Walters also into the shadow of the inland cliff.

"Now for it!" he whispered. "That's the fellow I sat on when we were starting. Oh! Look at them!"

The heaving mass that had burst through the elder bush, out of the cave, now broke apart. Instantly the boys recognized the two opponents, Bullet-head and the man with the pointed shoes. Though he had given the impression of being a weedy individual, a real townee and smart alec, he now showed something more. Those loosely carried limbs were powerful and fast. He was back on top of Bullet-head in an instant, throwing himself like a wet sack over this smaller adversary, who had taken him by surprise.

"Oh look," murmured Meaty again, still clutching the other two and holding them back, unseen. "We can't

114

do anything yet. I've got the rope here. I believe that boy can punish that thug, and I'll go in to help."

"You know who it is?" said John. "The man in the train. I wonder what's been happening here? Hobbs's pal is in a terrific rage. There! See that?"

Indeed he was. The man who had spread himself over the kneeling boy gasped, swore obscenely, and rolled aside. Bullet-head had rammed him amidships, making him lose breath. The boy was now on top and had caught the thug by the collar, twisting it and threatening to choke him. There were no rules to this game. Bullet-head, smarting under that rope's end, the humiliation of being tied up like a chicken, and the shock of seeing Hobbs so disgracefully exposed, now had his dander fully roused. And he was a born fighter. The build of his body and brain proclaimed that.

The fight might have ended there had not the elastic-limbed townee suddenly given a back kick that caught Bullet-head under the crotch, doubling him up with pain. This gave the other a moment's advantage, and he took it. With an effort he rolled over, jumped up, and was about to spring again on Bullet-head.

But the youth was also quick. He too jumped to his feet, and now the two faced each other in true fighting style, both gasping and sweating, but their fists raised for attack and defense.

Bullet-head went in first, and landed a left-hand cunningly, almost on the spot where he had butted the bully. It proved to be only a glancing blow, for the man had turned aside as he flung his right fist with a straight blow at Bullet-head's jaw. The boy appeared to be made of steel, for though he took the knock squarely, he just shook his head, blinked, gulped, and an instant later stooped, to bring an upper cut under the man's defense, drawing blood from that thin, ugly mouth.

Another bout of blasphemy, followed by some treacherous footwork aimed at Bullet-head's vital parts. But the boy was too quick. Leaping back, he paused for breath, while the other wiped a hand across his bleeding mouth. Walters saw the ring flash in the sun, to confirm his recognition of the man in the train.

"What do we do?" he whispered to Meaty. He was trembling. He had never before seen fundamental violence, humans turned into beasts of the jungle.

"Wait," said Meaty, who was used to the slaughter house. "That blighter won't stay the course. He'll cut and run when he sees a chance, the rat! There! See that? They're at it again!"

The thug, so far from running, had followed after Bullet-head and attacked with flailing blows, one of which took the boy on the cheek, avenging the blood-stained mouth. Both opponents were now bleeding, and Bullet-head hovered, irresolute and dazed.

That was where the thug made his mistake. He stayed close in, and tried another head blow; but Bullet-head, quickly recovering, saw it on its way, ducked, caught the arm between both his, and gave it a swift twist—not a sporting act, but an effective one, for it made the man overreach and stumble forward, bent almost double.

Bullet-head, freeing his hands with lightning speed, got in a thunderous blow on the man's ear that changed the course of his approach to the ground, making him roll and fall sideways.

The boy was on him at once, jumping with both feet on the small of his back.

Every evil now broke loose, and the onlookers had to give some admiration to the townee. Tortured by these latest blows, he still showed a quick recovery, seizing Bullet-head's ankle and wrenching the leg almost out of that tough body. Then he was on top, and an instant later had snatched up a bit of loose rock.

"No!" shouted Meaty. "No! No!"

He darted forward, the others at his heels, all yelling in terror.

The man turned, and saw the large figure of Meaty swinging the rope like a lasso. It was too much for him. With an oath, blood spurting from his mouth, he jumped up, letting the rock fall harmlessly on Bullet-head's back, and before Meaty could reach him he had leaped across in front of the elder bush and disappeared into the cave.

Meaty stopped, put his arms around the prostrate and breathless warrior, and lifted him to his feet.

"D'you see that? The devil was going to brain you with it!"

He picked up the lump of rock and offered it to Bullet-head, who now stood, gasping, the blood beading on his broken cheek, his eyes blazing with fury.

"Where is he?"

"Safe enough," said John Walters. "He's doubled back into the cave."

"Oh Lord, the others are there, still tied up! I had no time to release them. There were three men, though. Where are the rest?"

"Must be the fellows who've taken the launch," said Reynolds, "bringing bales to the landing stage."

"Bringing?" growled Bullet-head. "Not a bit of it. What's happened is this: We've broken in on their hiding place, and they don't know what to do about it. That's why we had such rough handling—touch of the rope's end, and kicked back into the cave, where they tied us up, while they planned to lift the stuff and take it back to the ship."

"Smugglers!" gasped John Walters. "Oh, my eye! *That's* not what we came for."

"Nor did we," said Bullet-head, now in control of his breath.

118

"My young brother's got the first-aid kit," said Walters, watching the gouts of blood still oozing from Bullet-head's cheek.

"Where's he, then?"

"One of our party has wrenched his ankle, so we've left them in the cave."

"Well, I wouldn't trust that slippery type near any of them, your lot or ours. He's in a foul mood. Taking up a bit of rock like that! It would have been the end of you," said Meaty, looking at Bullet-head with admiration. "You put up a show!"

They grinned at each other, worthy opponents, worthy friends henceforth.

"We're wasting time, though I had to take a breather," said Bullet-head. "Better go after him, and bring those other fellows out. Hobbs is in poor shape."

"I'll bet he is," said Reynolds dryly. He had been thinking, and now had more to say. "We'd better not all go in. You see, there's the other exit by the landing stage. That means the man has a chance of getting away. He can't get up to the farther entrance because the ledge is crumbled away. But I suspect that the hole where we've left our two fellows leads out to this entrance; which means he can follow it and get away to the landing stage. Besides, there are some parcels standing there, waiting for the next journey. We thought they were being landed!"

"I'll go back and watch the entrance and the landing stage," said Meaty. "It's my turn to take the next beating. And I'll have a bite of something while I'm waiting. That fight has given me an appetite. You want a morsel of something?"

Only Bullet-head accepted, as though to perfect the understanding between him and Meaty. He took a sandwich, and began to bite it. With a grimace of pain he groaned, and put the back of his hand to his jaw.

"I'd forgotten!" he said. "Well, that reminds me. Come along, then! We'll split up as you say—what's your name?"

"Sanders."

"That's right. And the rest of you. Pity we didn't join up from the start."

"We should have missed that grand fight," said Meaty eying the wasted sandwich ruefully as Bullet-head, after another futile and painful effort, flung it into the marshy reeds.

"The first thing is to release your friends," said George. "But then what?"

"What? We have to find that blackguard. He's a public danger," said Bullet-head.

"But look here," said George, "we're not exactly on a desert island."

"No, we can't take the law into our own hands," added John.

Both Bullet-head and Meaty laughed, looking at each other to share what they took as a funny little joke: those two solemn owls, Reynolds and Walters, wearing the responsibilities of civilized society.

"And how!" said Bullet-head, tenderly licking his bruised lips.

"Well, I'll be seeing you," said Meaty, picking up his gear but passing the rope to Walters. "You may need this, if you find that ugly customer. He's still got some fight in him!"

He set off back to the landing stage.

"Come along, then," said Reynolds. "We'll lose no more time. But that fellow can't do much. He's really a fool to have gone back into the cave. I think he may have lost his head a bit, as a result of that round with you—"

"My name's Carstairs," said Bullet-head. "And the one with Hobbs is called Jones. Clever one, too. He knows the price of everything. If he saw those parcels, I'll bet he'd tell you what's in them."

"Well, he *will* see them," said Reynolds, "for this appears to be a kind of storehouse for smuggled goods. And we all came to look for a dead Roman!"

With laughter, tempered by caution, they crawled into the cave, and were quickly swallowed by the darkness.

12.

DEAD-END BOYS

Lightning Soames was determined not to surrender. He allowed the Tadpole to offer first aid to his grazed knee, but was not inclined to thank him. He looked down on the fuzzy head, which threw a still fuzzier shadow on the white wall of the tunnel, and he cursed his fate, which had reduced him to this inactivity and dependence on the youngster whose presence he had objected to from the start of the expedition.

"Don't bind it too tight!" he grumbled. "How d'you think I'm going to move?"

"Well, you won't move, anyway, with that ankle."

Andrew Walters puzzled him. He knew he was treating the kid outrageously, but he couldn't help it. There was something too nice about him. Any fool would fall for that charm, that quietness, and Lightning was going to be an exception, as indeed he was in most other matters. One had to make a stand somewhere.

"How d'you know I won't move? I'll move if I've a mind to. We can't stop here, anyway, like—like maggots under a stone. No headroom, no light. Far better to try to climb back, and follow the rest of the party."

"We can't reach the hole," said the Tadpole. "After that drop, you ought to remember. Look how far up it is!"

He flashed his light up the wall end behind them, and a tiny segment of the disk of light sloped off to the top of the hole, causing it to appear only the more remote. A miracle how he'd clambered down!

"And if your ankle is really damaged, you'll only make it worse by using it before my uncle has had a look."

"You sound quite sensible," hissed Lightning, through his teeth. He was really in pain, but refused to admit it. "Any other wise instructions?"

The light was not strong enough for him to see the effect of his sarcasm. The Tadpole did not reply. He was examining the position, trying to make a rough calculation of the slope downward toward the farther cave, to study the roughness of the path, and the head play. There was not much room, for after the deep drop at the butt end, with the hole at the top of it, this cross tunnel shrank quickly. It was even lower and narrower than the tunnel which it was supposed to join just before leading into the farther cave.

"It seems quiet now," the Tadpole said. "If you really

123

want to move, we might try to get along. I could crawl, while you ride on my back."

Lightning was furious. "Couple of fools we'd look! As though you could bear my weight. Really, Tadpole, you've got the cheek of a girl."

"I don't know any girls. Are they cheeky?"

"If you had seven sisters, you'd know the answer. However, you're doing your best. I think the knee's easing off a bit."

"But you can't walk?"

"I don't know. We'll make an effort. Depends how far it is, and how rough. But it can only be a few yards, as I see it from my recollection of the crawl last year, up the tunnel from the outer cave, past the place where we found the skull."

The Tadpole pondered on this for some minutes, while he attached to his person the minor gear which had been lowered to him by his brother John; the two mackintoshes, a flashlight battery, and a package of food.

"Well, we'll find somewhere more comfortable to eat. Looks as though we can venture forward, now there's nobody about."

"No. It must have been holiday makers just poking around, on their way somewhere," said Lightning. He liked to have the last word, if only to remind the Tadpole how much longer he had been in this world, and how much greater was his experience of the ways of it.

"Well, shall we make a start?" asked the Tadpole.

With that, he put his hands under Lightning's armpits and tried to heave him up, the crippled elder boy also trying to help himself. The result was a groan of pain quickly smothered.

It was smothered because a rival outburst of human distress, several voices mingled, came through the tunnel. It might have been somebody crying, and another person swearing.

The two boys lay still, pressed close together, the one-sided antagonism forgotten.

"Something wrong!" whispered Andrew. "I don't like rows." His voice trembled, and Lightning felt his eleven-year-old body shaking.

"Take it easy, kid," he muttered. "We couldn't have moved, anyway. My whole leg is useless. It's frightful when I try to stand. We'll wait here until something else turns up. They know about us, after all, so you needn't worry. Just leave it to me."

He was half pleased with this new turn of events, because the Tadpole's infant innocence stood revealed.

"Quiet, now."

But they were not to be allowed to escape attention in whatever drama was taking place. The distant, muffled sounds of tormented humanity ended in a shuffling, as of sacks being shifted, and this was crowned with an angry shout and imprecations, not distinguishable but coming nearer.

There followed a more local noise. It was somebody crawling along the tunnel. Then it stopped.

"He's reached the junction of the two tunnels," whispered Lightning. "That proves we're at the other end of the one we saw last year, and didn't take. Now what?"

They were soon to know. The scrabbling sound began again, and it grew louder. Muttered blasphemies and heavy breathing accompanied it. Whoever it might be, he had chosen the right-hand fork, leading to Lightning and Andrew.

"What do we do?"

"Nothing, Tadpole. Leave it to me. I believe it's somebody trying to hide, or get away. Hobbs is involved in this. We must put this one off the track. If it's one of Hobbs's friends, then they've had a row about something, and all we know is that we didn't want any of them to snatch our prizes. They've evidently got there first; but Hobbs is a fool and won't know how to search. That maybe is why they've quarreled."

"*If* they've quarreled," said Andrew, but only half-heartedly, for he still smelled violence in the air, and his whole nature hated it.

"Shut up!" snarled Lightning. "Trust your uncle," by which he didn't mean Dr. Walters.

The groping, gasping, cursing came nearer.

"Lights out!" whispered Lightning. "Whoever it is will pinch our flashlights if he wants to disable us. Put them away."

They pocketed them, and waited in the dark, while the unknown crawler approached. Suddenly a flicker of light, as forerunner, darted up the slope of the tunnel. It grew stronger, shook itself free like a fan opening, filled the whole tunnel, and lit up the two small boys crouched under the angle of the abrupt end, beneath the hole.

It was thus that Pointed-shoes found them. After the fight with Bullet-head, he had leapt into the entrance of the cave, paused awhile as he was not immediately being followed, striven hard to recapture his breath and ease the various pains inflicted during the struggle. Gathering himself together, but still in a murderous temper, he pushed on to the outer cave, in the hope of finding another exit. He saw Hobbs and Foxy still bound back to back, powerless because their wrists were tied behind them.

"Ah! You ——!" he snarled, with an explosion of filthy language which Foxy fully understood, it being his purpose to know everything, for future profit.

"Nice if you broke loose too, wouldn't it?" he said. "I'd like to know how that other one got out. Well, I've given him what he asked for, and if you young devils try any more tricks, I'll give you the same. And it hurts! Oh, it hurts! You should see your pal!"

Neither Hobbs nor Foxy could see the condition of Pointed-shoes, while he was gloating over them and making their bonds more secure. He trussed them closer together, and both groaned as the rope bit into their bodies. Foxy kept his face hidden to disguise the cunning and hatred in his shifty eyes. Hobbs was too terrified to look up. It was just as well, for Pointed-shoes was not a pretty sight.

Certainly the two smaller boys abandoned at the end of the tunnel were not encouraged by the spectacle, though it was only dimly seen in the half-darkness, the throwback of the beam searching the whitish roof of the tunnel.

Then the beam was turned full in their faces, and they were temporarily blinded.

"What the—?" growled a man's voice. It was thus that Pointed-shoes found himself confronted again by youngsters in a place where he didn't want to find them.

"Who are you?" The light flickered over them, as though searching for hidden arms.

Lightning felt young Andrew trembling, but this did not prevent the infant from being the one to answer.

"One of us is hurt. He may have broken his ankle."

The light settled on his fuzzy head.

"What the hell are you doing here, anyway?"

The question was so brutally put that neither boy replied. That made the man suspicious.

"Speak up, can't you? What you got to do with that other lot?"

"Nothing," said Lightning promptly. "We're just exploring, and have come in from up there." He pointed above his head to the hole, and the man turned the torchlight instantly toward it—a gesture of distrust. He grunted, and Lightning continued, the characteristic note of cheekiness returning to his voice as his quick wits realized that the man was on the run and very uncomfortable.

"Why, is that another way out?"

The eagerness of the inquiry further betrayed Mr. Pointed-shoes.

Now that the beam was turned upward and reflected from the white ceiling of the tunnel, it threw a glow that made the stranger visible. Andrew trembled still more and gave a little cry of dismay. Then he did something which made Lightning finally surrender to the innocence of the boy's personality, and to admit to himself that here was a display of true courage. For, conquering his dread of violence, Andrew forced himself to stare at the painful sight of the bloodstained face, distorted by rage and sheer badness, which the half-light made even more diabolical.

"You're hurt too," he said. "Look! We've got a first-

129

aid kit, and my uncle is a doctor. Let me put a bandage on your—"

"Shut up!" snapped Pointed-shoes. "No time to fool about! Got to get out of this trap somehow! Here, let me get up there. It goes on, don't it? Where's it come out?"

With that rough brushing aside of the Tadpole's brave effort to be a Good Samaritan, the man stepped over the boys and actually turned them aside with his foot, causing Lightning to take the weight on his damaged ankle. He cried out sharply.

"Sorry, kid!" muttered the man, half ashamed of himself but driven on by fear. "Damn dark; can't see what I'm doing. Want to get out of this, y'know."

"It's too small," said Lightning, somewhat mollified by the apology. "We're the only ones of our party who could get through."

"What? What? More of you?" cried the man, pausing with his arms flung up to find a hold for hoisting himself to the hole.

"Yes, but they'll have gone out by now," said Lightning, whose brain was beginning to work at its usual speed. "If you could get through the hole, you could follow them to the river."

"Oh, the river! That's all right by me."

This exclamation of relief was followed by a quick

scramble over the boys' heads. Pointed-shoes paused level with the hole, then thrust his head and trunk through, and began to try to work his way. But he stuck. His legs splayed out, searching for support. His muffled voice swore, and his struggles increased as he found he could go neither forward nor backward. From the violent movements of his legs, and the savagery of his language, it was evident that he was panicking.

"Now's the chance to tie him up," whispered Lightning.

"Oh, it's horrible," moaned the Tadpole.

"Ugh!" said Lightning, contemptuous of this softness. "But that might be a mistake. We still don't know who he is, and what it's all about. We might be committing an assault. Besides, Meaty took the other rope. Better to catch him by craft. I've got an idea. We'll mislead him, send him farther into the caves. That'll shake his morale, and also it'll play for time."

He raised his voice, addressing himself now to the man wedged in the hole.

"I told you so. Take our advice next time. Look, stop struggling, and breathe out so that you're as thin as can be. Then we'll hang on your legs and pull."

It wasn't easy, for Lightning had to lever himself up on one leg, clutching every available handhold on the wall, a knob of rock, a protruding flint, searching for them by the beam of the flashlight which he had brought into action again, after motioning to Andrew still to keep the second one concealed.

The struggle went on, the boys doing their best to help the crook. He floundered and cursed, milling his legs frantically as his panic increased, almost lifting the boys from the ground and causing Lightning to groan again and again as the violent movements threw the weight onto his ankle.

"Oh, you'll pay for this," he muttered to himself, "whoever you are, you wrong'un!"

Then suddenly the man broke free, and tumbled on top of the boys. Lightning yelled with pain.

"Shut up, can't you!" hissed the man, gasping for breath, and trying to drag his cheap, smart clothes into shape. "Bring everybody after us!"

"Why not?" said Lightning nastily. "What's wrong, anyway?"

"Never you mind, kid. There's a bit too much nosing about going on as it is. Those young devils down there—" He indicated with a dirty thumb the direction of the cave toward which Lightning and the Tadpole had been making their way before the accident.

"Well, we've helped to pull you out of the hole," said Lightning. "That's something to thank us for. Now what do you want?"

"And I can really put a first-aid plaster on your face,"

said the Tadpole, producing and opening the box with the red cross on its lid. "You must have banged your mouth in the dark."

"Bah!" The man spat angrily. "All I want is to get out of this, I'm in a mighty hurry. Got a lot to do—see?"

"Well," said Lightning, with an oily smoothness, "you can get out by the way we came in last year when we first explored the caves."

"Cough it up, then. Get on with it!"

"It's not easy to explain," said Lightning, doing some quick thinking at the same time. "If you go back to the cave, and follow up the river, away from the siphon, you'll see that it comes through from an inner siphon, whose wall we broke down last year. You can now walk through this, and need not dive. But you'll have to paddle, for the narrow little path is a kind of ledge about a foot under water, on the left-hand wall as you go in."

"What's all that?" said Pointed-shoes. "Can't see where you're treading, like?"

Obviously he didn't like, but he was desperate and would try any course to escape from the caves.

"That will lead you past the waterfall, which you skirt by keeping close to the wall, and then you carry on until you get to the pothole, where you connect with the ledge which leads to an opening onto the common."

133

Lightning did not explain that the connection from the bottom of the pothole to the upper ledge was a matter of seventy or more vertical feet.

Pointed-shoes grasped eagerly at this means of escape. "Just the ticket!" he cried. "Out by the back door, eh boys?"

The prospect cheered him enormously, and he collected Hobbs's torch, which he had left on a rock bracket beside the hole, and without further consideration for the plight of the two small boys, and the fact that as far as he knew they were being left in absolute darkness, he began to crawl back down the tunnel, with a parting: "I'll be seeing you!"

The boys waited until the last muffled sound died away down the tunnel. Then Lightning produced his flashlight and lit up the dead end, a spot all the happier after the departure of Pointed-shoes.

"Better keep your light in reserve," said Lightning. "We may have to wait here a long time." He chuckled. "That little effort will keep him busy; but he'll be back, and none the sweeter. We ought to move before that happens. But we've time to eat something first. Then we'll try to get down to the cave and see what's been going on there. He's obviously met Hobbs's party, because he said something about 'what, more of you?'"

The two boys considered this while they looked into the bag of food supplied by Meaty. Munching eagerly, they found themselves with renewed courage. A quarter of an hour later, they set off slowly down the tunnel, Lightning in front, carefully shuffling along on his seat, the damaged leg held out in front like a bowsprit, supported by his two hands. The Tadpole followed, carrying the gear.

13.

THE INVISIBLE FOE

Pointed-shoes was pleased with himself. He left the tunnel and stood erect in the cave, stretching his cramped bones, which were also aching after the fright. But he was a quick recoverer, a faculty he shared with sewer rats. "Phew!" He stood under the overhanging wall of the cave and threw a shrewd glance or two at the trussed-up couple close to his feet. Neither dared to say a word, either of entreaty or threat of future justice. Hobbs, indeed, was reduced to abject ruin. His body shook, from time to time, with dry sobs, and this caused Foxy to shake too, his sullen face frowning at the nerve-racking reminder of their humiliation and misery.

Pointed-shoes appeared to be considering them while he groped about his disheveled person to find a cigarette and a match. He struck the match in cupped hands and held it to the damaged fag. The sly face was lighted up for a moment, the mouth and chin darkened and distorted by a scrawl of congealed blood. One eye was puffed.

136

Hobbs must have seen this, for his body missed a sob, then resumed the dismal rhythm. Pointed-shoes might also have seen himself had that not been impossible, for he had no sooner taken a puff at his cigarette than he exclaimed with disgust and stubbed it out on the wall, putting it behind his ear as from habit.

"Gawd!" he exclaimed. And with that he flashed his way across the cave to the stream, knelt down, and bathed his battered face in the icy water, uttering little groans of satisfaction at the healthy sting of it.

"Now for it," he muttered, half to himself. "You young devils! You stay pretty, see? Teach you not to poke your nose in other people's game, eh? You can wait till your pal comes around. And that won't be for some time, after what I've done to him!"

Hobbs shook still more violently, and Foxy's head sank deeper into his shoulders, self-protective and sulky.

Pointed-shoes, a dim shape behind the beam of his flashlight, followed up the stream, stopped to examine the opened siphon, then took off his shoes and socks, stepped across, and began to wade along the submerged ledge which John Walters and Lightning had explored in the opposite direction a year before.

He didn't like the cold water and greeted it with an expletive or two, lifting up one foot, then the other, as the cold rushed up his shins. Muttering to himself, he began to pick his way nervously along the submerged ledge, feeling with bare toes and flinching whenever they touched a sharp edge of rock or a protruding knob. Hell and all its attributes were called upon freely, to give him false courage. He balanced himself with one hand against the wall, leaning away from the stream for fear he might fall into it. In the other hand he carried his flashlight—or rather, Hobbs's, a large rubber affair like a truncheon. His own, having given out, had been left in the cave. He was not the kind of character who keeps things in reserve, or has a care for the morrow. Easy come, easy go, was his motto. He lived like the birds.

His progress was slow. Each step was taken gingerly, accompanied by convulsive workings of that damaged mouth, to signify his extreme distaste for this part of the adventure. However, at the back of his mind, which was not very far, lay the satisfaction of being able to dodge the gang of youngsters who had interfered with the day's work. He told himself, while groping ankle deep, every step an apprehension, that it was a lucky day after all, since the Customs men, in their drab black boat, were not on the scene too. These kids, after all, could be taken at their face value for what they said they were, just fooling around looking for old bones out of the past; some stuff they'd heard about on the radio, no doubt. He sneered in the darkness, contemptuous of everything outside his range.

138

Yard by yard he crept along, trying to keep steady, one hand grasping at holds upon the slimy wall, the light held above his head except when he dropped his aching arm to rest it, so that the beam should spread in as wide a circle as possible, enabling him to look ahead for snags and to keep a suspicious eye on that stream—a treacherous-looking surface too quiet, too swift to be trusted.

Once or twice he stopped and looked back. But the tunnel had curved, and he could not see the place where he had left the cave. Nothing behind or before him but the low tunnel, the level flow of silent water (except for its rhythmic breathing, or so it seemed, with a flicker here and there like a sleeping tiger opening its eye and closing it again), the greeny-white walls gleaming in the light of the torch; nothing but this scene, and the loneliness, the sense of being deep down, cut off from the world and from life itself.

Pointed-shoes stopped. He was shivering. The cold had begun to creep up his legs. His stock of oaths was running out, and he could only repeat the old ones. They were losing their strength and no longer reassured him or maintained his self-confidence. He wished he had *really* laid out that young college tough, who might by now be up to further mischief. Well, that was a problem for the two in the boat to face. After all, they were deeper in this game than he—always the poor stooge, as he told himself, the one who took the risks while the other fellow took the profits and the swag. You could trust nobody in this world.

He was really sorry for himself—no new thing; but now it was accompanied by misgiving, another approach to panic. Still, those two younger kids were innocent enough. Imagine offering him a bandage! The idea made him chuckle and that restored his belief in himself.

He groped forward again, and the sound of the underground waterfall suddenly floated into his consciousness. It had been humming and thrumming all the time, but as an undertone, and he hadn't noticed it. His nerves and senses were tuned only for things that were emphatic. He was a citizen of the kingdom of noise, and only at home there.

It was a relief, therefore, to hear something definite. The tunnel curved again, and widened, to make a frame over the ridge where the water slid, in a kind of metallic comb, on which the flashlight beam picked, throwing a prism of oily rainbow tints above it. With hardly a flicker or break in the beat, the flood curved and fell into the basin.

It was from this basin that the noise came—the seething, the frothing, the beating, a mass of confused waters that swirled backward, reaching like an angry tongue around and over the place against the wall where Pointed-shoes knew he had to wade.

He stopped and looked. It was a nasty sight. He might have been walking into a cauldron of snakes. "Phew!" he whistled, to keep his courage up, and he longed for a pull at a cigarette. But he dared not free his hands, the one from the confidence of the wall, the other from the leadership of the flashlight. He might stumble, or drop the light. The mere thought made his legs colder. The icy caress was up to his knees now.

He decided to push on and to get out of the stream as quickly as possible. He removed his left hand from the wall for a moment, to make sure that his shoes and socks were still safely secured around his neck.

It had to be faced, that whirlpool seething and writhing between him and the higher stand where the floor of the tunnel rose, and with it the ledge which left the stream. How safe, how warm and visible!

He hitched his shoes closer around his neck, put out his hand again to feel the slimy wall, winced at the contact, and moved forward: one step—two—three. Then at the fourth he felt no bottom. The ledge broke under water.

With a sharp gasp he drew in his breath and swore. That was a near one! He might have gone down into that deathtrap! Gingerly he groped about with his right foot, leaning sideways to the wall for fear of overbalancing and tumbling into the flood.

The light trembled in his right hand, and the veil of

oily transparencies in front of the waterfall trembled too, sending up a flight of light-petals fluttering around the walls and ceiling of the tunnel, as though an autumn wind were blowing over a forest of glass. But these ghost shapes, shattered from the prism, made no tinkling sound. They were silence itself adding nothing to the rush and miniature roar of the waters.

Pointed-shoes began to talk to himself—never a good sign.

"Come on, you silly—" he muttered, loading himself with a leaden expletive, as though he had not enough to carry. And on he went, having by now found that the break in the ledge was only a narrow one over which he could step, so long as he took care to lean inward to the wall and trust his weight on the hand in contact there.

He was over. A moment's pause, just to be sure, and he moved on again. The serpents of foam were seething around his shins now, beating and snicking at the skin with tiny invisible teeth. But no harm. It was only in play. He reached the edge, and was able to relieve himself of the light and his footwear, which he put out of harm's way on the path above and well back.

Then he grasped the edge and began to heave himself up and out of the icy grasp of the water. But his right hand slipped. He had clasped a shade, or rather a thin protrusion of rock that broke in his grip. He lurched to the right, bruising his already painful ribs against the edge of the rock, and nearly pitching into the center of the snake pit of waters.

But he saved himself; or at least his once-smart suit saved him by rucking up into a thick pad that caught him against the edge and held him there, for just sufficient time for him to find a second and safe grip. But the waters claimed his fountain pen, which shot out of the pocket of his jacket like a pea from the pod and sank. He saw it disappear. He swore, then forgot it. Nothing mattered so long as he got out of this place. And things were easy to come by, after all. He didn't have to earn them by hard work, like the rest of the mugs. Oh no!

Resting on the dry path, he felt quite pleased with himself and could afford to pause for a smoke at last. All was plain sailing now, according to that kid. Just carry on past the waterfall until he came to the pothole that led to the way out.

Puffing contentedly at his fag, feeling the warmth gradually returning to his numbed feet, Pointed-shoes pondered vaguely on what a pothole might be. He hadn't come across that one before: something new in his very varied experiences as a free lance of fortune. However, that was all right. He'd soon find out, on his *way* out too! He felt really *good*.

He was not interested in the scene before him: the

six-foot plunge of the fall; the great knots and bosses of rock bruised by time and water into every color of the rainbow; the cluster of fungi coagulated close to the river's edge on the farther side of the pool. His attention was fixed on the certainty that now he could get away safely, leaving his two companions to deal with the problem caused by the boys' stumbling on the hiding place for the contraband. He knew the risks of this interruption of the well-laid plan. The sooner those parcels were removed inland, the better for all concerned: the skipper and crew of the tramp steamer, the men engaged in the landing and transport of the goods, and the Boss in the City. Only one person in that organization really interested Pointed-shoes. That person was now sitting pretty, beside an underground waterfall, believing himself to be on his way out to safety, leaving police and customs agents prowling up and down the coast.

Pointed-shoes chuckled, and in doing so caused his cracked lip to remind him of the recent narrow escape. He flinched, grinned and flinched again, then got up stiffly, having drawn on his socks and shoes.

He could now see where he was treading; most reassuring after the hazards of that stretch of underwater exploration.

The tunnel curved to the left, and not until he had passed this curve did Pointed-shoes come to the small arena, the bottom of the pothole where John Walters had landed after that grim descent on the end of the swinging and twisting rope, and had stared across the stream at the ruby-tinted eye of the toad.

Pointed-shoes flashed his torch around the larger space, looking for the promised way out. Once, twice, three times the beam probed the darkness, but it found no break in the dome.

Then the fugitive reached the center of the well bottom. He was beginning to be uneasy. There was no way ahead, for the stream seemed to come in from nowhere. The path had ended. What next?

The beam of the torch went exploring again, and it trembled a little.

"Eh?" exclaimed Pointed-shoes suddenly, and aloud. He had heard a sound from above. Directing the beam vertically, he saw the pothole above his head. Up went the shaft, vanishing in funnel-shaped perspective to nothingness, to darkness.

He stared up, trying to find what he knew was impossible—a way out. Not that way. No! The kid could not have meant that way. He must have spoken of a continuation of the path, out at the farther side of this ghastly dome—somewhere by the spot where the stream came through.

He approached the water's edge and followed along until he stood face to face with the wall. The stream flowed in through a long, broken slit or flaw at the base of the wall, some six feet long, spreading out to fill the shallow bed along which it flowed so smoothly and quietly. There was no other opening.

Pointed-shoes had been tricked.

For a minute or two his mind refused to realize it. He searched again for a way out, but the effort was half-hearted.

"That little devil!" he said half aloud; he would have enlarged on the exclamation had not the sound of his own voice in that dreadful place startled and subdued him. The words fell like slabs of lead from his bruised mouth.

He began to breathe hard. He could hear his lungs at work. That wouldn't do. He must keep a firm hold, take another look up that shaft. Perhaps the way out was through a hole some feet up, like the one where he had found the two youngsters who had directed him to this place.

He searched upward again, staring with his head thrown back. Suddenly a heavy and icy weight struck his forehead, nearly stunning him and making him stumble. It was a drop of water, one of the momentary drips from the condensation down the shaft.

"Oh, my Gawd!" he cried aloud; and the heavy words fell dead at his feet.

Recovering his balance, but still breathing hard, he turned in the other direction. Perhaps the way out was across the stream. His light went searching yet again. It flashed on the smooth surface of the water, picking out a highlight here and there as the rhythm of the movement broke. Then he saw something which almost stopped his labored breathing. It was a beady eye.

He was so startled that his hand involuntarily flicked the beam upward to the roof—or lack of roof. Then, slowly, he searched for the object again. Yes! There it was, glinting at him across the river. He stared. It stared back. It was the jewel in the head of a huge toad, a squat, bloated, shapeless beast as hideous as that bunch of fungi which he was only now conscious of having noticed beside the waterfall.

He stared, fascinated by disgust. The toad did not move. It was either indifferent or contemptuous. There was no offer of help in that ruby eye. Pointed-shoes had met his match, and slowly he accepted the fact. He knew there was no way out. The shaft above his head went up to infinity, for all he knew. There was no hole, no path, no escape.

"Now look here!" he began, addressing the toad. But the toad did not even blink. It might have been a lump of misshapen rock, except that a faint rise and fall along its underside indicated life; half animal, half mineral. It breathed, and it breathed with a deadly regularity; unlike Pointed-shoes, who by now was making odd little noises as he sucked the stagnant air into his frightened body, and expelled it again as useless to help him out of this dilemma.

"Better go back," he muttered at last, and he turned with loathing from his fruitless address to the toad. Slowly, reluctantly with yet another despairing flash round the bottom of the pothole, he began to retrace his footsteps along the tunnel toward the waterfall.

He paused there to remove his socks and shoes, and to try to think out what he should do when he got back to the cave where those two boys were still tied up. Would the third one, with whom he had fought, have released them? But they would know he was trapped here, for it was now obvious that the other two kids crouching in that blind alley were members of the same racket.

Pointed-shoes could not think seriously about these problems, however. All he knew was that he must get out to the open air. But even this desperate need failed to prevent him from shuddering with fear as he lowered himself to the submerged path beside the waterfall, where the backwash formed.

He now had to lean to the right instead of to the left, and this meant that he must hold the light in his left hand. Slowly he picked his way, feeling with a bare foot at each step. He had not taken a dozen paces before he trod on a sharp edge of rock in the hidden ledge. He recoiled and glanced up at the hand pressed against the wall of the cave. He saw the flash of the stone in the ring on his finger, and that familiar sign of pride almost restored his confidence.

"Good luck!" he murmured, and started to move forward again. But the jerk upward of his head must have strained the laces of his shoes, or perhaps he had not secured them in a firm bow. Suddenly they gave way, and with a loud plop his shoes and socks fell into the water.

He had no time even to swear. Bringing his right hand away from the wall, he stooped and groped in the icy water: but he could not see or feel. Then he flashed the light into the stream at his feet, and saw one shoe on the ledge, and the other dimly, lying at the bottom, changing its shape under the distortion of the flowing water.

First he tried to grasp the shoe that flickered and wavered in the stream, but it was deeper down than it appeared to be. He saw his hand elongated, reaching down vainly. He felt the cold too, and both saw and felt the ring slide off his shrinking finger, to fall through the depth of the water in an almost living movement, as though it were a bright minnow with flickering fins.

This was disaster. Pointed-shoes depended on that ring. It was his badge of confidence. It stood for his way of life. Now it was gone.

He crouched there, as low as he could without submerging himself in the water. He almost prayed for the ring to come back, to rise by a miracle from the spot, some four or five feet out, where it had settled on the pebbled bed of the river, gradually growing more dim as particles of sand gathered around it—sand and grit, mineral cousins to the flashing stone in the gold band; how much less, yet how much more!

Somehow or other, Pointed-shoes succeeded in fishing up both shoes, after a despairing effort. The socks inside them were sodden and he could not wring them out here, for there was no place to put down the light safely.

By the time he had tied the shoes together again, and decided how he should carry this dripping burden, his ring had disappeared under the crowding particles of mineral stuff swirling in the stream and along the bottom. He could not even locate the spot where it lay buried.

Angry and fearful under the superstition of this loss, Pointed-shoes moved on. His craving to escape was still in command. Nor anger, cunning, nor fear could hold him from this urgent need to get out of the caves, no matter what might follow.

He slopped along, no longer able to support himself against the wall, the light held before him, the shoes in a dripping bundle in the other hand—the hand that lacked the ring.

"I'll pay 'em!" he cried out suddenly, his rage mastering his sanity. He was hardly conscious of what he meant. Vaguely, savagely, he was striking out against human society, and beyond that at some force even more indifferent and vast, the force that made these waters flow, these cavern walls close about him like a trap. Life, for him, had always been a trap which he had been smart enough to evade. But now it had nipped him. He was frightened. He floundered on. It hadn't quite got him, and he was fighting his way out—in the only way he knew, with a kind of rat courage.

At last he reached the siphon where the stream entered the cave. By some mechanical turn of the mind, he remembered to step across the break in the submerged path before stepping out to the dry shelf that opened onto the floor of the cave.

Instantly, saved from that ordeal by water, he realized that he might now have to confront these youngsters, probably all three of them. He snapped off his light and listened.

Nothing. No sound except the whispering of the stream, telling itself its own secrets with little chuckles of delight.

Pointed-shoes took two or three side-steps up and away from the river, his back pressed against the cavern wall, his arms spread and feeling the way. He was breathing fast, and he tried to control the noise of his panting. He was not yet sure. Those boys might be around. They might even have found help.

He waited a little longer. There was still no human

sound. If those two boys were still tied up where he had left them, in the dark, they would have betrayed the fact by now: a sigh, a movement. But there was nothing.

He flashed on the light, but the battery was giving out and the light was dim. It was enough to show that the cave was empty.

So they'd been released and were gone. But where were they gone? Before his reviving brain could answer this question, he saw the spade belonging to Hobbs's party. He was so excited by this discovery that he did not pause to ask himself how the tool had been removed from the farther tunnel to the wall of the cave under the broken gallery, where the boys had been tied up.

Pointed-shoes (though mis-named thus, because the sodden shoes were still a burden in his hand) picked his way across the sandy floor, took up the spade, and made his way along the tunnel.

"I'll knock the daylights out of that kid!" he told himself. He was in a murderous mood, and pictured the two smaller boys whose false directions had let him in for that horrible adventure farther along the underground world, and the loss of his ring. He pictured them still waiting at the top of the right-hand tunnel for their friends to find them.

He was not very clear about it. He did not stop to

consider if the other boys, with the tough one from outside, might have joined them. He was determined to punish those kids, and that was all he could think about, except for the still clamoring need to get out of the caves. The spade promised him help in that matter. He believed he could enlarge the hole into which he had thrust himself, and so get out by the way in which he believed those boys had entered.

He turned right at the junction and began to crawl forward, having secured his shoes to the spade handle. Time was giving out with the battery, and he would soon be plunged into darkness. He switched off, to save the last of the battery, and groped his way by feeling: a simple task in so confined a space.

So he reached the end of the tunnel; and by that time he was almost relieved to find that the boys were gone.

"I might have killed those little devils," he said to himself. "Just as well I've missed 'em!"

With that kindly thought, he switched on his light again and began to hack away at the hole above his head. The sides were shaley and brittle. He quickly made the opening large enough to allow him to pass through.

This success reassured him. He felt warmer after the exertion, and warmth promotes courage. Without waiting to put on his shoes (for they were still sodden) he followed the failing light of the lamp, passing down the cave in the direction where he believed the main river must lie.

His anger and fear were still heavy about him, but now there were hope, relief, even certainty of escape. He believed he would be out of this place in a few minutes. And after that he would lose little more time before clearing out of the neighborhood of the coast, back to the safety of the City. There would be some explaining to do when he saw the Boss and the two fellows with whom he was working. But that was easy. He could always think up a tale. Indeed, facts spoke for themselves today. Would anybody else have done better?

He was beginning to be pleased with himself once more, in spite of the loss of his ring and the discomfort of his battered face and bare feet.

With confidence renewed, he congratulated himself for a clever fellow when he saw daylight at the spot where he had hoped it would be. If he had not been so weary, footsore and bruised, he would have hurried forward to that promise of daylight and certain escape. Instead, he limped toward the light, short of breath, and stumbling where his bare feet encountered loose stones and treacherous patches of shifting sand.

And there, in the entrance, he saw a fat boy, a tough-

154

looking youngster almost man-size, stirring out of sleep.

It was too late for Pointed-shoes to draw back. He was desperate. Anything was welcome after that experience in the caves. His quick wits made him decide to bluff a way out.

"Hullo, chum!" he cried, trying to appear hearty and carefree. "Lost my way in the caves, like. Am I right for the jetty by the river?"

But his voice was hoarse and uncertain, almost as feeble as his appearance.

Meaty Sanders got up, turned and stared at him coolly. He saw the man who had fought with Hobbs's friend. The poor wretch was now a bedraggled figure, dripping wet, stained with slimy sand, his face pale and distorted by a smear of dried blood which gave him a woebegone expression. His hands were bleached and sodden. One of them held the flashlight, and its dying beam still gleamed in the bright sunlight. He was too confused to switch it off. There was not much fight left in him.

Much must have happened outside since Meaty left his companions and walked back to guard this entrance to the caves, for now he stepped toward Pointed-shoes, barring the way out, and before replying gave a long, loud whistle through his teeth. Then he replied, "Yes, you're right for the jetty."

And as he spoke, an answering whistle came from that direction.

"Here, what's your game?" said Pointed-shoes. "Who've you got down there?"

14.

A JOINING OF FORCES

LIGHTNING SOAMES and the Tadpole did not get far down the tunnel before they had to stop. The effort was too much even for Lightning's dogged temper. He moaned, and sat down in his tracks so suddenly that the Tadpole butted into him.

"I can't do it," he exclaimed, prepared to blame the Tadpole. "But if that thug comes back on us I don't know what will happen—!"

They sat in silence for a few moments, Lightning struggling with the pain and trying to nurse his leg in the darkness.

"We've *got* to get out of this tunnel!" said Lightning at last, more exasperated than ever. "Can't you see that?"

"Can't see anything in this darkness," replied the Tadpole, so reasonably that Lightning's impatience was fanned into flame.

"Idiot!" he cried. "You know what I mean!"

"Yes. And I'll tell you what," said the Tadpole. He sounded as though he were thinking things out quietly. "It's simple enough. We'll go pony fashion. I'll be the pony, and you can ride on my back as I crawl forward. We don't need to hurry. You stick your leg out straight, and I'll keep to one side so there's no danger of banging it against the other wall. That's the way, Lightning."

"What, a kid *your* size, carrying *me?*"

The Tadpole ignored this gibe. He switched on his own light, and got busy shifting the gear, most of it being now disposed by him about the person of his passenger. Lightning, helpless with pain and baffled pride, had to surrender.

"All right," he grumbled. "You'll never hear the last of this, you brat!"

A grin, half friendly, half hostile, flickered across his face, to be revealed by the beam of the Tadpole's flashlight.

"Come on now," said that urchin, crouching on all fours, while Lightning carefully mounted, with the injured leg held stiffly forward like the lance of a jousting knight in armor.

Thus they progressed, inch by inch. The Tadpole found the weight enough to punish his knees badly as he crept along the uneven floor of the tunnel.

"Sorry!"

Lightning had groaned as the Tadpole dipped with

one knee going down into a hollow, causing the stiff leg to jolt against the wall.

"You wait till all this is over!" he growled. But there was no malice in his voice. He was beginning to revise his opinion of John Walters' young brother. However, he had to groan again, and keep up the pretense of teaching this kid not to become too big for his boots.

"Carry on," he said, as though giving orders to a very humble lieutenant.

And the tiny cavalcade moved on again, Lightning gingerly balancing himself so that his foot should not suffer too much, and the Tadpole thrusting his head up and back, to pick his way without stumbling. The flash-light was in Lightning's hand, just another imposition put upon his dignity by the small boy who was now in command of the situation.

They made an amusing spectacle as they emerged from the tunnel into the cave, to be greeted by the united party of John Walters, George Reynolds and Bullet-head Carstairs, who had meanwhile released the two miserable figures of Alan Hobbs and Foxy Jones from their humiliating bondage back to back in the darkness, under the sloping ledge from the upper entrance near the top of the cave.

John was busy, with the help of Reynolds, rubbing life back into the cramped limbs of the two prisoners, while Bullet-head, bidden by Reynolds, was helping them to sandwiches from the store supplied by Aunt Mary.

Amid this activity, a cry from Lightning made them all turn.

"Good heavens! That kid's done well!" exclaimed Bullet-head.

Indeed, the Tadpole was nearly collapsing. Both his knees were raw, and the last few yards between the junction of the tunnels and the entry to the cave had been conquered only by sheer will power—a faculty in which that fuzzy head was not lacking, as Lightning might now be prepared to acknowledge.

He did not say much, after being lifted off his steed and set comfortably down on a cushion of sand. Reynolds, while listening to the tale of Lightning's misadventure, was examining the ankle with intelligent fingers.

"There's nothing broken," he said coolly. "You sprained it, stretched a ligament."

"Listen to the fellow who lives with a doctor," grumbled Lightning, still sore at being humbled. He hated being fussed over. It reminded him of that army of elder sisters.

John took the Tadpole in charge, conducting him to the water's edge and bathing the grazed knees, a process that caused the young hero to stamp and roar in protest.

When peace returned and hunger had been satisfied,

a council was held with George Reynolds in charge. While he was putting his plans to the now united party, John Walters studied him with affectionate interest, thinking to himself that this shy, stooping figure would not have taken command so naturally as this a year ago, though even then something in his character had brought him forward as leader after the shameful collapse of Alan Hobbs.

That fine fellow, at this moment, was rapidly regaining confidence in himself, but he had been too effectively abased to make a full comeback. He too studied Reynolds (his next-door neighbor with whom he had little contact) and there was no affection in his glance, nor one gleam of gratitude at having been rescued from the recent humiliation. Indeed, he felt only the more aggrieved. But he could say or do nothing, for he was still badly shaken, and he ate the sandwiches as though they were made of brimstone rather than good brown bread, butter and ham. Shame is a poor sauce to any meal.

"Well," said Reynolds, "we've not got very far with our main purpose, the search for Roman remains. All this nonsense with these town types is done with, I hope, though that fellow who shot back into the caves here must be lurking somewhere."

"Surely," cried Lightning, who was lying on the soft sand piled against the wall, having had his foot securely bound up by Reynolds—a job that failed to make it possible for him to walk. "I led him astray very nicely! I told him there was a way out at the back of the main cave. But I didn't say that he would have to climb up that seventy-foot funnel to get to it."

"But even then he couldn't get to it," said John Walters, who saw no joke in this trick but preferred to deal with facts alone. "You forget the breakdown of the ledge!"

"So I do," said Lightning, with such a comic grimace that the whole committee laughed—except Foxy, who never laughed at anything, and Alan Hobbs, whose pride was beginning to take command again, urging him to stand apart from the rest of mankind, wherever he might be, in order to prove his superiority.

"What I suggest is," said Reynolds, pausing to think, "that we take Lightning out to the open, and he can wait there comfortably until we see what the situation is about the speedboat. After all, Hobbs, those strangers are not likely to make off with it. They couldn't get away with that, knowing how the Channel Police are always on patrol, and how well-known your father is in the district."

He put that last bit in as a tonic to restore Hobbs's self-esteem, mistakenly believing that he needed such mental medicine. Hobbs responded instantly. He put on his leader-of-men attitude, though John Walters could see in his eyes a slightly uncertain look, due no doubt to the explanation to be made later in the day to Hobbs Senior about the unsanctioned loan of the *Speed Queen*: an explanation painfully similar to that which Alan had to make a year ago, in the matter of the smashed electric lamp.

"Let's get going," said Bullet-head. "We've eaten all your grub." He grinned at Walters, to show his appreciation.

"What about leaving the top entrance unguarded?" asked Hobbs. "I want to make sure of getting that brute."

"Why, we're not leaving it," said Lightning. "I'll be squatting there while you go for—"

"And first we want to rake over that bit of floor where the skull lay," said Reynolds. "You never know."

Nobody had time to ask what he meant, for Bullet-head, tired of so much talk and inaction, had begun to sort out the gear, and to improvise a means of dragging Lightning up the tunnel to the open air by a couple of mackintoshes tied to the rope, to be pulled by the two stoutest members of the united party.

In this practical matter Hobbs was not consulted, and therefore he ignored what was being done and gave himself to general supervision and issuing of orders which nobody obeyed, not even Foxy Jones.

The contrivance worked, and Lightning was pulled

163

along the tunnel, grumbling at the bumps and jolts. A halt was called at the widening in the tunnel.

"Where's the spade?" said Hobbs. "You had it, Jones!" he cried, turning sharply on Foxy. "Go back and get it!"

Foxy didn't move. He was thinking about that dangerous character lurking somewhere among the caves. Nor was he quite so certain about Hobbs's position as self-constituted captain of the expedition. He wanted to make sure about that before he declared his allegiance.

"Go on!" said Hobbs angrily.

But young Andrew, the Tadpole, had already disappeared. During his absence, Reynolds moved up and down the floor, testing it by prodding with his foot.

"There's something here," he said.

"Look, it's only an inch or two down."

Bullet-head, with hands nearly as broad as spades, went down on his knees and scooped away the sand, to reveal the top of a parcel wrapped in waterproof.

"It's the same as those two down on the jetty," cried John. "Oh boy! What have we found?"

The only member not wildly excited was George Reynolds.

"We've not found what we came for," he said, drily. "This may be dramatic, but it's not Roman remains!"

"Hard luck, Professor," said Bullet-head, who ap-

164

peared to have taken a liking to Reynolds. "Now I hope that laddie with the nimble feet will have to come back to pick up this luggage, since he can't escape by any other way."

At that moment the Tadpole reappeared.

"Where's the spade?" said Hobbs.

"It's gone. And d'you know, I heard him!"

He told them how he had passed the junction of the tunnels on his way to the cave, and was stopped by the sound of somebody crawling up the blind tunnel, grunting as he went.

"And you went on to the cave?" said Lightning.

"Yes."

"Foolhardy idiot! He might have come back and caught you."

One of Bullet-head's large and sand-soiled hands clapped the Tadpole on the back.

"I had to see if the spade was there," said the Tadpole, addressing himself to Reynolds rather than to Hobbs.

Before anything more could be said, or done, a distant sound came from the interior.

"That'll be the thing breaking through the small hole with the spade," said Lightning. "He's trying to get out to the entrance by the jetty, where Meaty is waiting for him."

"Suppose we follow up?" said Bullet-head. "That customer is still very ugly—and by now he'll be desperate."

With that, they decided to leave the parcel buried in the sand while they dragged Lightning out to the open, made him comfortable in the shade of the elder bush, and hurried along under the cliff toward the other entrance.

15.

THE BATTLE OF THE JETTY

Meaty was glad to be alone, for he was ravenously hungry. One or two odd sandwiches, snatched during the morning, failed to nourish his huge frame. And to eat continuously in front of the other members of the club made him feel mean. He could not understand why the rest of mankind showed so mild an interest in good food.

He stopped on his way between the two entrances to the caves, and leaning with his back to the cliff and the stretch of marshland in front of him, facing the open Channel, he unhitched his haversack and set to in earnest, polishing off half a dozen meat sandwiches (the best cut from his father's sides of beef), a couple of tomatoes, and an outsize cooking apple.

"Ah!" he said, wiping his fingers on his trousers. He would have said still more, only there was nobody to say it to, and he had a dislike for being laughed at, even by sea gulls and choughs, spectators of the feast and

167

none too friendly because of the small share they had been given.

He could have enjoyed a nap, and he would have had one, but for the feeling that he ought to get to the entrance by the jetty, to watch events there. So he merely yawned and stretched his mighty arms aloft, as though to say, "I feel fine!"

He was about to step along the path when he saw the customs launch, with its little blue flag at the stern, appear around the coast, coming down-Channel.

Instantly he was alert. Like his father, the butcher, Meaty Sanders was a man of action. He whipped out a grubby handkerchief and, after waving it wildly to attract attention, began to spell out words in morse code. "Come to the Jetty. Important!" he signaled.

From the distant boat there came a flash of light. One of the customs men was replying with a hand mirror. "O.K." it said; and Meaty saw the boat slowly turning close to the shore, nosing its way to the jetty. Those customs watchdogs knew the coast as well as they knew the backs of their hands.

Meaty did not hurry. He had calculated that by walking with due consideration for the snack he had just consumed, he would reach the jetty at the same time as the boat. He was right. The black prow of the Revenue launch slowed and stopped, letting the ripples die away as an officer seated beside the man at the wheel spoke.

"What is it, son?"

Meaty was sleepy, and the story was long. How was he to begin?

"Anything amiss?" said the officer impatiently.

"Well," said Meaty, "there's been a fight; and there are these parcels here. I don't know whether they're coming or going."

The officer stood up and eyed the two parcels. Then he frowned at the fat boy, puzzled by his slowness.

"What d'you mean—a fight? Who's been fighting, and where?"

"At the other entrance to the caves," replied Meaty, who was still trying to get his story straight, with first things first. The effort made him yawn, an achievement that heightened the officer's impatience.

"Oh, for Heaven's sake, boy, cough it up. What are you trying to tell us?"

"Well, there are two gangs this year, our lot, and Hobbs's. It's Hobbs who owns the speedboat, or his father does. And the smart alecs, three of them, have pinched the boat, to carry away, or bring in, these packages. And one of them was outside the other entrance to the caves, when one of Hobbs's gang jumped out and there was a fight, which—"

169

"Now wait a minute. One of the packages was outside *what* other entrance of *what* caves?"

"No, one of the three men, I mean. And one of our party recognized him as a member of a gang who've come to the coast in an old racing car, driving dangerously and nearly putting Dr. Walters' wife into the hedge. He's the one in the fight. It looks as though some dirty work is being done. The others are out now in the Channel, in Hobbs's speedboat."

Meaty's effort died away. He was hopelessly entangled in his own words. He wanted to explain that it was an urgent job. His agitation explained more than his confused speech. The officer ordered his man to draw in. Jumping out, he examined the outside of the packages.

"No labels," he said. "Looks like German packing. Something fishy, eh?"

He turned to Meaty.

"Look here, my boy, you and your friends may be doing the Crown a service. I don't know about these caves. You say there are two entrances?"

"No, three," said Meaty. "And the man we had a fight with ran back into the caves. He's lurking around now. The other members of our gang have gone in after him, and the only way he could possibly get out is by this one, for the third can't be got at from below, since the explosion."

"What explosion?"

Meaty grinned. "That's another story. You see, we're looking for Roman remains, and all this other business has come as a surprise."

"And you think these chaps are landing stuff here, without papers?"

"Or they might be taking it back to the ship, owing to our having disturbed them."

"Oh, I see, hiding the stuff in the caves until they can get it away by road? That's the little game?"

The officer studied Meaty for a few moments, then spoke decisively.

"Look here, young man. I propose to disappear again, leaving you here. I want to see what their next move may be. That's a Swedish boat in the Channel, bringing in mine timbers. I think we'll call in the River Police on this. You can look after yourself here, I take it?"

He had observed Meaty's muscular limbs. Meaty grinned again.

"Try me!" he said. "That skunk nearly brained Hobbs's friend with a lump of rock, after getting the worst of the fight."

"Oh, it was as serious as that? I see! Well, we'll make ourselves scarce, and lie back under the shore just behind the bend of the coast while we put out a radio message. If your man appears, and you are in trouble, give us a whistle. We'll leave the parcels here at present, until I can ask somebody a few questions about them. Is that all clear, my boy?"

With that, the customs launch put off again, drawing close under the shadow of the cliffs and disappearing round the bend. Meaty watched it, and saw the officer at work on the walky-talky instrument, with earphones over his head.

With a smile of satisfaction and sleepiness, Meaty retreated to the mouth of the cave behind the elder bush, and settled down to wait upon events. He lay with his back to the wall, and dozed off.

It might have been a few moments or half an hour later that he was wakened by the sound of Pointed-shoes stumbling out of the tunnel. The greeting, which led to Meaty giving a loud whistle through his teeth, quickly took a nasty turn. The man, who by now was desperate, advanced on the boy with an intimidating glare of rage and frustration. He had been through enough, and did not intend to be caught at this late stage.

Meaty stared at the cunning face, pallid and bruised, with the snarl of the loose lips increased by the streak of dried blood which the adventure in the underground river had not fully washed away. After the greeting already described, Pointed-shoes turned nasty.

"You're the fool who tried to rope me down, eh?"

Meaty said nothing. He waited.

172

"I hadn't spotted that!" said the man. "Now I recognize you. What's your little game, eh? Trying to follow me around?"

Meaty gave another shrill whistle. It added to the man's fury.

"Shut that!" he shouted, and lunged forward, intending to strike Meaty across the mouth.

The man-size boy raised both arms like a bar across his face, knocking up the blow. Then he laughed—a deep belly-chuckle of sheer animal excitement.

"No rocks this time," he said, suddenly jumping forward and seizing the barefooted man by clasping both arms around him. "You don't brain me, as you tried with the other chap."

Pointed-shoes was surprised by this massive attack. He had little strength left. But with a last effort he pretended to collapse and fall to the ground, bringing Meaty down with him. Then he wriggled aside, broke out of the young giant's clasp, and would have bounded away had not the boy been quick enough to seize him by the bare ankle, which he twisted so firmly that the man was thrown again.

There followed a wrestling match in the course of which Pointed-shoes found a reserve of strength, for he struggled like a cat, writhing and striking out with all the cunning he could summon from his tired brain and body.

Meaty, however, was fresh. And he believed that re-inforcements were on the way. After a while his weight and muscle began to tell, and he held the man down.

"Cut it out, chum," gasped Pointed-shoes, with Meaty sitting on him and holding him face down, with his arms pinioned behind his back. "Will you take a couple o' quid?"

"You might have killed that fellow, after a fair fight too," was Meaty's reply. "We'll wait here now for the police, who are looking for you. And here they are!"

The words were no sooner spoken than Meaty was seized from behind and dragged off his opponent. Turning quickly, he saw two men, one of whom had him by the back of his jersey.

"Asking for trouble, aren't you?" said that worthy, a seaman with a cast in one eye. The other man, frowning and aloof, spoke next, addressing himself to Pointed-shoes.

"What's all this? You look done in. Where've you been, and what's brought this youngster here? We want no more witnesses and time's slipping away with the tide."

Pointed-shoes, relieved at first, was now angry. "Witnesses! D'you think I like them? A blasted boy at every turn I take! Been trying to get away from them ever since you put off with that first load, and—"

174

"Shut up. Don't advertise what we're doing. The thing is, what to do with this boy while we get the stuff safely away. It'll have to be downriver to the City with the last load. Not safe to ship it again. And no time to lose. We'll tie this cub down! Whip his jersey off, Jemmy, and make sure of him with it."

But Jemmy had not reckoned on Meaty's well-nourished fists. One of them landed on his diaphragm, winding him and making him leave hold of the back of Meaty's jersey.

A second later, the boy's other fist landed on Jemmy's jaw, felling him. There were still two men to one boy however, and now they attacked, the third man with contemptuous, long-range indifference that left the job to Pointed-shoes, who, again like a cat, had taken a new lease of springlike energy. He jumped at Meaty, who stepped back to the wall beside the entrance, thus protecting himself from the rear.

But he could not last long, even so, for Jemmy was now up again, and three dangerous, determined assailants rushed the boy. He hit out and caught the disdainful leader a blow as he leaned forward to close with the boy. The sneer on that cold face turned to rage. Meaty was in for a bad time now. Another feint and lunge repelled Jemmy, but meanwhile Pointed-shoes had jumped aside and pulled down a branch, thick with foliage, across Meaty's line of vision, temporarily blinding him. The leader took advantage of this, and brought the boy down with a side punch.

"Got him!" gasped Jemmy, with a twinkle in his crooked eye. "The young varmint!"

This remark was followed by a thud and the flying back of the branch of elder to its natural position as Pointed-shoes fell across Meaty's prostrate body. Bullet-head had returned to the battle.

What happened during the following few minutes, or it may have been hours, cannot be fully recorded. All was noise and confusion. The leader of the men tried to shout the boys down, for he aimed at attracting as little notice as possible. He cried out, pleading for a reasonable talk about the situation. But the cast-eyed mariner and the fear-maddened Pointed-shoes were too desperately engaged by Bullet-head and Meaty Sanders to be drawn off.

"Get that kid away," gasped Meaty to John Walters. "No place for him."

Nor was it the place for the demoralized Alan Hobbs, who at the sight of battle had decided that his mission was to seek his father's speedboat and ensure its safety.

"Go with him," said John to the Tadpole. But the small boy was reluctant and had darted in to help

Meaty, who was now engaged with the sailor, giving blow for blow.

John, standing helplessly as an onlooker because of his short sight, knowing that if his spectacles were knocked off he could see to do nothing, had to watch his young brother rush into the fight.

"Come out, Andrew," he cried, in agony. But Andrew had already taken a flying leap onto the back of the sailor, to cling there and clasp his arms around the man's head, blindfolding him by this embrace. This gave Meaty the opportunity either to close with his opponent or to knock him out. Andrew was in danger of being hurt, whether Meaty floored his man or the sailor forced Meaty back and gave his attention to the small tormentor on his back.

John and George Reynolds, both detesting the whole brutal business, had to watch through this moment of poised conflict, their attention being drawn also to the fight still raging between Bullet-head and Pointed-shoes —a savage fight because of the suspended anger of the boy and the fear in the dazed mind of the bully. Like John and Reynolds, the third man, the leader of the gang, looked on irresolutely, also hating the struggle but for other reasons. He foresaw nothing but disaster for his purpose, and the next few minutes proved that he was right.

Before Andrew could be swept aside like a terrier from a baited bear, and before Pointed-shoes and Bullet-head could determine who should receive the knockout blow, there came a sudden interruption from outside.

The customs officer, followed by half a dozen River Police, ran forward. They had just landed, drawn by the sound of the scuffle. They had waited round the bend of the cliffs, to see the *Speed Queen* return from the Swedish ship out in midstream. Allowing time for the men to land, the customs launch, now joined by the police boat summoned by radio, made for the jetty. The government men saw what was happening just above it, under the shadow of the bushes and the cliff where the entrance to the caves lay concealed.

"Time!" shouted the customs officer, vastly amused by the pluck of this group of youngsters, and not a little pleased by the results of their interference in the affairs of the grownups.

The fight stopped instantly, as though the combatants had been touched by a magic wand of sleep. There they stood, frozen in the attitudes of strife, arrested by surprise.

Pointed-shoes was the first to break the spell. He stepped back, and was about to disappear through the hole behind the elder bush. But he was too late. Not even his town-and-gutter cunning could survive such a day of misadventure. George Reynolds had slipped between him and the cave, and stood there, gaunt and severe—but really rather bored and nervous—like a forbidding angel.

Here was a creature, both in appearance and in mood, beyond the comprehension of poor Pointed-shoes. The man's spirit broke. He turned in a complete circle, looking at the ring of police, the boys, the whole structure of human society against which he had spent his life, as at a power that owed him a grudge. He almost whimpered.

"Okay," he said. "You don't have to tell me."

"No," said the customs officer quietly. "It's you who are going to tell me."

But in speaking, he turned instinctively to the third man, knowing by experience who would be the leader of this tough trio.

"The goods you're handling: I'd like to see the bills of lading and the rest of your papers. Got them handy?"

"And the matter of assault?" added the police sergeant. "Who began this fight? And where do these lads come in?"

"That's it," said Pointed-shoes, while his leader frowned at him as a signal to give nothing away. "Look at my lip. That's what they done to me! I want to give that guy into custody," pointing venomously at Bullethead, who had joined Meaty and stood looking on calmly, undisturbed by the pummeling he had been given. "That's who started it."

"Is that so?" said the sergeant. "The boy down in the boat—who says you stole it, by the way—has a different version. He said something about being jumped on in the caves, tied up and left there in the dark. D'you know anything about that, by any chance?"

"My word's as good as a kid's, ain't it?" whined Pointed-shoes, lugubriously lifting a bare foot and nursing it in his hand, tottering in the process. "Never had a chance, I haven't. Always been up against it."

"Yes," said the sergeant. "You've been down this way before, I fancy. We begin to feel quite sorry for you. It's not the first seaside holiday you've had spoiled."

He turned to the customs officer.

"Shall we go along, sir? We'll take the names and addresses of these lads, for the court may want to thank them publicly. They've done a good day's work."

"Indeed you have," said the customs officer. It was George Reynolds whom he patted on the back, though that peace-loving worthy had taken only a passive part in the encounter with the intruders on the archeological expedition.

After the formalities and further congratulations, the boys were told that they would be hearing more in due course, and that now they were free to pursue their original plans.

"That's not so easy," said George, somewhat rue-fully. "You see, there's still some stuff buried in the sand where we had intended to dig; and also there's the matter of the speedboat."

"What about the boat? You've got it back, haven't you? We shall take all that into account when these fellows come up before the Bench."

"Yes," put in Foxy Jones, who had been a mere quivering onlooker during the fight, "but Mr. Hobbs, who owns it, ought to be compensated. He didn't know his son had borrowed it, and if it's damaged in any way—"

"Oh, *borrowed* it, did you?" grinned the sergeant.

"No, I didn't. It was Hobbs, his son. That's what is worrying. Something ought to be done about paying an adequate rate—"

"Cut it out, Jones," growled Bullet-head. "The government doesn't do things like that."

"But Hobbs has got to balance matters with his father," said Foxy, almost weighing the pros and cons on his fingers and long, questing nose. "You've got to have equity."

His anxiety, however, did no more than amuse the rest of the now united Tomahawk Club. Meaty and Bullet-head hardly understood what he was talking about; they were too busy tidying themselves, removing traces of the battle.

The customs officer, however, was sufficiently im-

181

pressed to make a suggestion. "Well, as we're going off by boat, you had better come down to the jetty while we take these gentlemen away, and you can examine the speedboat for yourselves. Which of you is Hobbs?"

"He's gone down there already," said John Walters.

"What! While the fight was on?"

"Yes."

"Oh, I see!"

The officer and the police sergeant looked at each other. The former put his hand on the Tadpole's shoulder.

"And how small is Hobbs? As small as you?"

Nobody replied, and both Bullet-head and Foxy Jones looked uncomfortable, as though they were ashamed of something.

Pointed-shoes was allowed to put on his footwear, and then the three men were escorted to the jetty; only a few yards, but the procession was slow and stately, the smugglers in the midst of the police, followed by the customs officer, with the boys in the rear.

There, sure enough, was Alan Hobbs, in the prow of the *Speed Queen*, leaning over and painfully trying to sponge away the marks acquired during the trip out to the Swedish ship. But scratches and abrasions cannot be removed with a sponge, and Alan Hobbs knew that he was laboring in vain. When he saw the party approaching he looked up, and the expression on his face was one of utter despair and fright.

"It's all serene, my boy, the fight's over," said the officer dryly.

Hobbs flinched. "They've knocked the boat about," he said. "My guv'nor will be mad."

"I've claimed compensations," put in Foxy.

"That won't do me any good," said Hobbs, more frightened than ever.

"You have our sympathy," said the officer, still more dryly. Then he turned to George Reynolds.

"We'll be sending up some help over those excavations. You say there are more parcels? I hope they haven't disturbed the sleeping Romans too roughly. However, you carry on, and if you find signs of the twentieth century, as well as of the fourth, you can put them aside for us to collect later in the day."

The police, with their prisoners, embarked, and the customs officer, having had the two parcels from the jetty lifted into the Revenue launch, pushed off also. The boys watched the two vessels speeding out down-Channel toward the City.

16.

AS YOU WERE

WHAT ABOUT IT?" said George, at last. "We've wasted most of the day over this affair. And young Lightning has to be got home somehow. He's not good for much."

"Just the ticket," said Meaty. "Hobbs can take him back in the speedboat, and put things right with his old man."

"Oh, can I!" cried Hobbs. "You don't know him. When he sees the damage those brutes have done he'll go raving mad. They must have scraped it alongside the ship when they were unloading their wretched parcels. The cheek of it! If I had my way, I'd give them—"

"You've missed your chance," said Bullet-head. "But Sanders here, and I, and this kid, have done it for you."

Hobbs flushed with anger. "You can't expect—" he began.

"No, that was our mistake. We *did* expect. But now

184

the job is to bring that chap down from the other entrance and get him home."

"That'll take too long," said Hobbs, still under the cloud of fear. "I might manage to get back before my guv'nor, if I speed up—and there might be a chance to paint out these marks before he sees the boat. I'm off now."

He would have pushed out, as he was still alone in the boat, had not Bullet-head seized the painter.

"Oh no. That's a cad's trick, Hobbs. If your father is back, Jones will talk him round. Come on, out you come."

Hobbs sulked, but he had to obey. He was also obliged to go with them along the undercliff path, so that he could not make off with the boat while they were bringing Lightning Soames down to the jetty.

That impatient sentinel at the farther entrance to the caves was in no way grateful when the other members of the Tomahawk Club arrived to rescue him.

"What's going on? I've missed everything! I heard the row, but I couldn't move. Unfair, all you fellows enjoying a scrap, while I have to stick around here bored to death, and—hallo, what's the matter with Hobbs?"

"Be quiet, Lightning," said John Walters. "Don't stick your neck out, as well as your ankle. Hobbs is taking you back in the *Speed Queen*. That's all you need to know."

"Here, what's the mystery? I'm missing something."

He would not consent to be moved unless he was told the whole story, so while Bullet-head and Meaty were carrying him along to the jetty, followed by a sulky Hobbs, the rest of the party gave him the history of the fight and the arrival of the customs men and police. The Tadpole had little to say. He had probably forgotten what had happened, for all his interest, indeed his passion, was concentrated on the *Speed Queen*, just as it had been fastened on the little station wagon when Aunt Mary picked up him and his brother at the station.

"Hobbs will run you directly to the landing stage at the bottom of our garden," said Reynolds to Lightning.

The Tadpole heard this. "I say! Can I come with you? Can I?"

He ignored the fact that Hobbs was walking by himself, his sulky fears wrapped around him like a cloak of gloom. The small boy's worship, however, snatched that cloak aside, and Hobbs looked at him with mild interest and patronage. Something belonging to him—at least, to his father—was attracting attention. That made him feel good and restored his self-confidence.

"You'll have to obey orders," he muttered, putting

on an official frown. Here was a chance to resume command. In this mood he began to superintend the transport of Lightning Soames into the boat, and the last that was seen of him, as the *Speed Queen* sprang into life and moved off with the Tadpole's fuzzy head sticking up in the prow like a figurehead, was the disdainful skipper with one arm flung negligently over the tiller, his head and glance averted from the four boys remaining on the jetty. He appeared not to have noticed the fact that his two guests and schoolfellows had deserted him, though it had been suggested that Foxy Jones should go back to plead for him, when the trouble began, over the damage done to the boat.

George Reynolds, after a stealthy glance at Bullet-head and Foxy, took the small sketch book from his pocket and made a quick drawing of the diminishing boat, which was making at high speed for the open Channel before turning to disappear up the larger tributary that ran past the gardens of the houses suburban to the town.

Bullet-head watched Reynolds in silence. He was awe-stricken, not so much by the skill of the draughtsman as by the calm and detached serenity with which he could turn from a recent rough-and-tumble with a gang of smugglers to this steady-handed interest in the shape and movement of a boat, the curve of its wake widening out over a net of broken sun reflections, and the over-biding peace of the great water and the summer afternoon.

"What do we do here?" Bullet-head whispered at last, nodding toward the artist as though to give his bewildered question more point.

"It's okay," said John. "He won't be a minute. And its worth recording."

Bullet-head shook himself, like a dog waking from sleep. "I wish he'd recorded that leap."

"What leap?"

"Your young brother, when he took a flying angel onto that johnny's back just as Meaty was about to be knocked into the middle of next week. Why, that tough could have taken us on all together, and with one hand. But your kid blindfolded him—did you see?"

"I don't know," said John. "It's a beastly business. Let's forget it. We didn't come here for that sort of thing."

Bullet-head grinned and looked from Walters to Reynolds, and back from Reynolds to Walters. His low forehead wrinkled in perplexity.

"You're an odd lot," he said, slowly. "Can't make you out. You really mean you *want* to forget it?"

It was Reynolds who answered. Though concentrated on his drawing, he had overheard this conversation between Walters and Bullet-head. Slapping his sketch book shut, and snapping the elastic band around it, he turned briskly to the party at large.

"That's about right," he said. "We're free to get on with the *real* job now, after all that interference. So let's return to the tunnel and look for what the Romans buried there nearly two thousand years ago."

"Will there be treasure, as well as bones?" asked Foxy, his eyes lighting up.

"You never know," said John Walters. "But we'll go and find out."

"Wait a minute," cried Meaty Sanders. "Wait a minute. What about a bite of something before we start? Still got some grub left at the bottom of my nosebag!"